THE THREE-TWO PITCH

THE
Three-Two PITCH

A BRONC BURNETT STORY

BY *Wilfred McCormick*

GROSSET & DUNLAP · PUBLISHERS

New York

Contents

TO MY FATHER

DR. I. B. McCORMICK

a fan who thinks baseball games should
begin at sunrise and end with the sunset

THE THREE-TWO PITCH

Chapter I

A PITCHER IS BORN

Top of the eighth!

From where he sat, cross-legged, half hidden between two cars parked well down the left-field foul line, sixteen-year-old Bronc Burnett saw his Sonora teammates hustle onto the field without him. For the hundredth time that awful afternoon it made him swallow—hard—seeing them out there, and another boy in his place.

Their endless chatter echoed and re-echoed from the towering, forest-clad canyon walls behind:

"Still eight to seven! Let's hold 'em, gang! That's the old fight! What do you say in there, Pitch? We've got a one-run lead . . . big as a house! Let's get number one. . . ."

Bronc Burnett, watching almost numbly from the side line, raised the bill of his cap. He rubbed a grimy sleeve across his forehead, then for the dozenth time in the last thirty minutes, he pulled the cap so low that his steel-gray eyes barely showed beneath it. He reached down and jerked a blade of grass from between his knees, chewing at it savagely as he sat and watched.

"All right, let's get number one! Make him hit to me, Pitch! Everybody alive now. . . ."

The stands took up the bedlam. Hold 'em out there, boys! Only two innings to go, then a third straight win for little Sonora High. Against *Spur*, too! Last year Spur

3

had handed them an ignominious twelve-to-nothing shut-out. "LOCALS SCALP SONORA," the *Spur Daily Banner* had ridiculed.

Now the long shadows of early mountain dusk were soaking across the diamond as the first visiting hitter selected his bat and hurried to the box to start the eighth. A blast from the stands greeted him: some applause, a few handclaps, some catcalls—all an inseparable mixture that goes with American baseball, whether it be across the continent in Brooklyn, or here among the cowboys and mountain men of New Mexico.

Folks were on hand today. Everybody. And the crude, homemade stands of rough pine, built that past winter by eager volunteers in a baseball-hungry town, were packed to their fullest.

"Strike one!"

The Spur batsman had missed it a country mile.

Again the stands broke loose. So did a couple of dozen automobile horns. The Sonora catcher, a bulky figure in his mask, belly protector, and shin guards, strode out in front of home plate. He made the shortened toss to his pitcher, shook his clenched fist high above his head.

"Where's all the pepper, gang?" he shrieked furiously. "Now, everybody on his toes! Let's *go* out there!"

He hurried back behind the batter, went into his squat, flashed a signal to the pitcher, then crouched—ready.

"*Ball one!*" announced Sheriff Pole Drinkwater, acting as umpire. "Too far outside!" A murmur of protest rippled through the crowd.

"Never mind that in there, Pitch! Still way ahead of him, boy! Still way ahead of—"

Patrolling left field, directly in front of the spot where Bronc Burnett was sitting along the side line, a slim, thin-faced little youngster who couldn't have weighed more than a hundred and twenty pounds hunched forward importantly, with his hands on his knees. Bronc's position—

4

until today. But "Peedink" Harrell's now! Peedink, like Bronc, was a sophomore.

"Come on, Pitch!" the kid piped shrilly. "Only two more innings! Let's get it over with so we can go home!"

Bronc Burnett, hearing, grinned dryly. "Go home, your foot!" he muttered. "Why, you little squirt, you wouldn't swap left field for the best home in New Mexico!"

"Come on, Pitch! Make him hit to me."

This first hitter for the invading Spur nine was a big fellow. Right-handed. "Bucket" Baker, Bronc remembered . . . so called because of his incurable habit of stepping back with his left foot for each pitch. "Stepping into the bucket," they called it. Baker hadn't done much that afternoon. Fanned three times and grounded out to third once. Nevertheless, a couple of tremendous foul smashes on high inside balls had barely fallen outside the flag, far down this left-field line.

"Might straighten one out yet!" Bronc surmised grimly, as he saw the Sonora catcher raise his gloved target higher than usual. "Shouldn't pitch high and inside to this bozo. Looks like—"

Crack!

There it came. Not so hard hit this time, higher in the air, but soaring straight for left field.

"All yours, Peedink! Take your time. Nobody around! In the well, boy. . . ."

Peedink Harrell had started forward as the ball rose. Not far—perhaps three or four steps. But now, too late, he saw his error and was off balance. Valuable seconds passed as he recovered. He began backing up frantically. Then as the ball went over his head he made a desperate grab, tipped it, and missed. The ball hit a skinned place on the otherwise grassy turf, bounded freakishly high, then began to roll with "home run" written all over it.

Baker scored standing up. All tied now! Spur eight. Sonora eight.

The crowd jabbered noisily for a moment, then as all eyes returned to the diamond, a hush fell over the little grandstand. Out on the wings where folks watched from parked cars, right-angling along both first- and third-base foul lines, everything was quiet there, too. Everything except for the endless, inimitable jargon coming to them from the diamond:

"That's all right, Pitch! Oughta had the big one, sure, but never mind that! Let's get the next one! Everybody alive now."

A pudgy, fat-faced boy of sixteen came trotting along the side lines to Bronc. He wore a baseball cap and spiked shoes, but only a plain khaki shirt and pants for the simple reason that none of Sonora's extra uniforms would cover Fat Crompton's overly ample body.

Fat dropped to one knee beside Bronc. "Cap'n Al says for you to stay warmed up," he announced.

"I'm warm," Bronc replied stiffly.

"Not the way he wants you to be! Here—I've brought my mitt—I'll catch you!"

"You don't mean he wants me to pitch? Shucks! That home run wasn't the pitcher's fault! Peedink oughta caught that one in his pocket!"

"I didn't mean to pitch. As a matter of fact, Cap'n Al probably doesn't even know you can pitch. This is his first day with the team, you know. He just said for you to be ready in case Peedink muffs another one."

"I wonder why not now?"

Fat Crompton did not reply, but something in his manner caused Bronc to grip him sharply by the arm.

"Why doesn't he put me in now?"

"All right then, Mr. James Burnett, Jr., alias Bronc!" grinned Crompton. "You stuck out your chin—I'll hit it! Cap'n Al wants to leave Peedink in, if he can, because Peedink will be the first man to bat in our half."

Bronc grunted. "Bat—your foot! He hasn't swung at a pitch all day!"

6

"Maybe not, but he's got on base four straight times. Three walks and plunked in the ribs once. As for you—"

"I know!" Bronc interrupted grimly. "As for me, I've been to bat ten times in two games, according to Fibate Jones's figures, and I've never yet stuck my foot on first base. But Fibate didn't bother to tell our new coach about my twelve put-outs in the field, or the four men pegged out at home plate."

"I slipped word to him," Fat explained. "He knows, now. That's why he may want to use you defensively after Peedink bats this next time."

A grin of hope broke through Bronc Burnett's squarish features, as he picked up his glove and sprang easily to his lithe six feet. He motioned for Crompton to get ready.

"A little baseball is better than none, I reckon. Gee, Fat! I'd give an arm and half a leg to crash the line-up today!"

Fat Crompton hesitated momentarily while he struggled to force his thick left hand deep into the catcher's mitt. Then he glanced up. He forced a half smile, at the same time reaching out to lay a set of surprisingly strong fingers on Bronc's shoulders.

"Even if I wasn't a good detective by nature," he said, "I could still guess why you're taking it so hard today. It isn't really on account of little Peedink. It's your father, now, isn't it?"

Bronc nodded.

"Where is he—up in the grandstand?"

Again Bronc nodded. "Yeah. Up there somewhere, probably with a lump in his throat that he can't keep down. It's the first time he's had a chance to see me play. But let's get started!" the husky youngster added, almost savagely. "It'll make me feel better to cut loose with a few fast ones."

"That's the way to talk!"

Fat trotted off about sixty feet toward home plate,

paralleling the left-field line, turned, and socked a big fist into the pocket of his mitt. Bronc took a step forward, half pivoted, and threw him the ball. It had been an easy, careless motion, but the ball fairly zipped into Crompton's hands. Crompton grinned delightedly as he tossed it back.

"I'll bet you could throw a baseball through a two-inch plank!"

Bronc Burnett was not needed that inning. Bearing down now, the Sonora pitcher—a tall senior with three years' experience behind him—struck out the next Spur batter, watched his catcher grab a pop foul for the second out, and threw to first on an easy grounder to retire the third man.

The Sonora team trotted chattering to their bench.

"Nice going, Pitch! That's holding 'em! Now, let's get some runs, fellows!"

But the visitors, now that they were again in the ball game, were showing plenty of life too. Back and forth, over and across, they fired the ball to one another. Meanwhile, their pitcher made his five careful, deliberate warmup throws to the catcher. On the last, the catcher pegged beautifully to second. The second baseman tossed it to the shortstop, short to third, third to first, as the four nimble infielders clustered nearer about the pitcher. The first baseman rubbed the ball momentarily between his cupped hands, wiped it on his pants, then tossed it underhandedly to the boy waiting on the mound.

"Let's go in there, big fellow! Everybody behind you!"

The infielders scampered hastily back to positions.

"All right, let's go! Let's send Sonora to the unhappy hunting grounds! Who's the first victim in there?"

The stands bellowed approval as the first victim, little Peedink Harrell, came almost timidly toward the plate. He lugged a bat that seemed as large as his waist. But

8

that didn't matter—the pay-off wasn't on size! Maybe he was little, but he had a mortgage on first base! Four times already that day. The kid had a good eye, all right. A walk's just as good as a single!

Down on the left-field foul lines, Bronc Burnett paused in his throwing and stood with both hands on his hips to watch Peedink Harrell step into the batter's box. Peedink was crouching low, a tiny figure that looked almost pitifully frail beside the big Spur catcher and the lanky umpire.

"I'm glad I don't have to pitch to the little cuss," Bronc conceded. "The way he stands there, a pitcher's only got a target about the size of a milk bucket."

The crowd roared delightedly as "Ball one!" streaked across the plate a trifle high. Then "Ball two!"—a shade low.

Suddenly the pitcher stepped forward from the mound. He beckoned to his catcher, then took a few additional steps to join him for a brief conference. They both stood watching little Peedink for a moment, then the catcher slapped his pitcher on the back, turned, and trotted back to position.

The strategy was quickly obvious. They were going to *make* Peedink hit.

The pitcher took only a half windup. Then, with deliberate aim, he tossed a half-speed pitch straight for the heart of the plate. Peedink rose to the bait, all right, swung his big bat with all his strength—and connected. It was a lazy "blooper," floating tantalizingly just back over the first baseman's head for a clean single.

The crowd responded with a simultaneous blast that shook the diamond itself. Out on the mound the Spur pitcher stamped disgustedly.

"Did you ever see anything like it?" Fat yelled at Bronc. "That puts him on first five straight times today!"

Bronc bit his lip. He had been on the verge of retort-

9

ing: "That shouldn't have been a hit at all! The first baseman was way out of position—playing too close in—should have been an easy out!"

But Bronc fought the impulse aside. He began putting more and more into his warmup.

What the heck—no use building a grudge against Peedink—let the little cuss have his day! He can't hold the pace, anyhow. Next week will show him up in practice, as Cap'n Al gets acquainted with the squad. Smart old ballplayer, that Cap'n Al. Lucky he's bought a little ranch here in Sonora—lucky for us, especially with our regular coach gone for the season. Wait till Cap'n Al sees me drag down those long flies next week! Just wait—I'll show him! And I'll get my hitting eye, too. Then I'll be back in left field. And the next time Dad comes in to see his son play . . .

There! It's a long one! It looks like—it is! It's a *hit!* Good old Smitty, sure laid the hickory to that one. Now we've got Peedink camped on third, and Smitty on first. Nobody down.

Now we'll get a run, and then you can bet Cap'n Al will put me in left field to protect the margin for the last inning. That's sound baseball. Cap'n Al knows the game; couldn't have played shortstop eight years in the big show if he hadn't. Yeah, he's cagey, all right. I'm slated to take over left field this last inning, and, brother, watch me show Dad! I'll show 'em all!

Bronc would have rated 50 per cent on his diagnosis of the game.

Peedink *did* score a run that sent Sonora ahead nine to eight. A beautiful double by Bill Burnham was responsible—after two were down, too, as "Slow Molasses" Smitty had been plucked off first base, and Red Bailey had struck out. But as the inning closed, and Sonora hustled onto the field to protect their thin lead in the ninth, little Peedink Harrell was the first to race into position.

Bronc noticed. Then he turned to stare at the Sonora bench. But there was no signal to him from Cap'n Al.

"Batter up—play ball!" ordered the umpire.

Again the burst of applause. More honking. Again the steady chatter from the loosely nervous boys on the diamond.

"That's enough, Fat!" Bronc called to his catcher.

He motioned for Fat to keep the ball and strode frowning over to his former spot between the two cars, and threw his glove on the ground. Still benched. Benched in favor of a spindle-legged little shaver he could stick in his pocket. That wasn't good baseball—a coach ought to play percentages. Suppose this Spur outfit knocked a couple of flies to left? Suppose Peedink lost the game for Sonora? Then he wouldn't be such a hero.

But, shucks! It wasn't Peedink's fault—Peedink was just following orders. If they lost now, it would be on Cap'n Al's head. Right where it belonged, too. Cap'n Al ought to realize that a coach should field his strongest *defensive* team with a one-run lead in the ninth. Everybody knows that! Peedink ought to be yanked out of there. He's done his part—he's already earned a big write-up in tomorrow's *Sonora Messenger*. Now, why doesn't Cap'n Al put somebody in there who can catch a ball?

The first Spur batter, plainly overanxious, struck out on three successive pitches.

"That's the way to chuck in there! Got the big one out of the way, Pitch! Everybody alive now. Make the next one hit to me, boy! Make him hit to me. . . ."

The next hitter was a big, red-faced fellow, who stepped to the left-hand side of the plate. He took a good stance; well back, feet about parallel, swinging his bat easily as if it were a toothpick.

"There goes my chance to get into the ball game," Bronc muttered gloomily to himself. "That big left-hander will never hit to Peedink. Most likely toward right. There! Cap'n Al is shifting the team over. Shucks —why doesn't—"

Ball one!

The big fellow had watched an outside low one zip past.

Ball two!

Again he had refused to nibble. The next one would have to be in there. Either it would, or he'd have the Sonora pitcher in a bad hole. The crowd sensed it too. A buzz of low, excited talk swept through the stands. Then a hush, as they saw pitcher and batsman eye one another momentarily. The pitcher deadly serious. The batter grinning confidently. Now the pitch:

Crack . . . Snap!

The ball crashed straight back at the Sonora pitcher. He had seen it coming, impulsively stuck out his bare hand, knocked the ball down, then couldn't find it in time to throw out the runner.

"That's all right, Pitch! Never mind that, boy! Wait —what's the matter? His hand's bleeding! Hey, time out, Umps!"

Sonora's acting coach, "Cap'n Al" Carter, was first to reach the injured pitcher, who was now walking around in a small circle, his hand folded tightly up under the opposite armpit. He had lost his cap, and a tense frown plainly showed that he was in distress. Cap'n Al slipped a supporting arm around his waist, as a dozen others gathered closely about them.

Carter wasn't a big man, at first glance, but the more one studied him the more convincing he looked. Perhaps three inches shy of the six-foot mark, he was, neverthe-less, solid as a granite boulder, from his bulging shoulders down to a pair of unusually small feet, which gave a lithe, catlike spring to his walk. His arms were long, his hands enormous. He looked the genuine ex-leaguer, all right, the Al Carter who had captained the rampaging Sox back in the rough-and-tumble days of baseball.

He quickly jostled the crowd out of the way so Doc Esberg could get through to the injured pitcher, then called his team into a huddle.

When the accident had occurred, Bronc Burnett had leaped to his feet. But when he saw the general stampede toward the pitching mound, he halted, then slowly retraced his steps and sat down again. Nothing he could do that somebody else couldn't do better.

Wonder who they'll put in now? Lefty Lear, probably. Lear has a fair curve ball, but he's wild as all get out. Bad spot for an erratic chucker, too—only one away, and with the tying run already parked on first. Maybe they'll pull Red Bailey in from right field. Red had once mentioned that he used to pitch back in Oklahoma. Say, there was an idea! If they pulled Red in, who would take Red's place in right field?

Why, *he*, Bronc, of course!

There's the sensible thing to do. Red is the logical man to pitch them out of this hole. Sure, bring in Red! Bronc half rose to his feet, wondering if it would be all right to go and suggest it to the new coach. After all, Cap'n Al wouldn't know. He'd never seen the boys play before. Maybe he should—

What was that? His name?

Sure! Fat Crompton was calling. He could see now that the whole group had whirled and was looking in his direction.

"Come here, Burnett!" The coach's voice this time.

Bronc scrambled upright, hurrying forward. He'd show them how to play right field! Just let 'em hit to me, Red! I'll help you, boy!

He paused, panting slightly, before the coach.

Cap'n Al got right down to business. "Crompton, here, says you're a pitcher. Can you win this game for us?"

A pitcher? Bronc nearly swallowed his tongue. But his mind worked fast: the tying run on first, one man down, *his dad up there in the stands* . . .

"Sure, I can win it, Coach!" The words were out, almost before he knew it.

A slender, bookish-looking youngster of about seventeen, carrying a notebook in one hand and a pencil in the other, elbowed through to Cap'n Al's side. "Burnett has proved a disappointment so far this season," he said. "Ten times at bat, I have him listed, and neither a hit nor a walk. If I might suggest—"

"Hold your suggestions, Fibate!" Bronc interrupted. "We're talking about pitchers now—not batters!"

"Bronc can throw a baseball through a two-inch plank!" Fat Crompton put in eagerly. "More or less, of course! I know—we've been practicing every night for a week."

The coach had been eying Bronc closely. "You've got the build, all right," he muttered, half to himself. "Let's see your hands."

Bronc held them out, palms up, then turned them over.

"Good pair of hands, too. And you seem to have the confidence—a pitcher must have that."

"Then you're pitching me?" Bronc asked eagerly. "Sure, I've got confidence, if that's all you're worrying about."

A momentary hush was broken by Fibate Jones.

"It's conceit, rather than confidence! Why, if you ask me—"

"*I didn't!*" Cap'n Al snapped the words like grasshoppers jumping from a bait can.

"As far as that's concerned," he went on, "I wouldn't give a dime a bushel for ballplayers without confidence. They're always cocky—the good ones. Maybe not obnoxious about it, and maybe it's sometimes hard to find.

14

But it's there. Always! Confidence enables a ballplayer to relax—to be at his best in a pinch.

"And another thing," the coach continued, as a motion from Fibate indicated he might interrupt. "From this point on, I'm wearing the pants around here. I had to go a little slow at first because I didn't know a thing about any of you. But from now on—and particularly next week when we start real practice on real baseball—I'll be giving the orders. All of them! Understand?"

There was a moment of silence. Then, almost quietly: "You're the chucker, Burnett! Good luck to you, lad!"

Bronc felt the hot blood rush to his face. He swallowed hard, stood riveted for an instant longer, then as his teammates melted away from him and a roar broke from the stands, he stepped over to the pitching mound. He was all alone now. Gee! A baseball diamond was a big place. It looked like a mile over to first, where Smitty—or was it Smitty? Whoever it was, he looked blurred and unnatural.

Suddenly his knees felt wobbly. What had he got himself into, anyhow? He'd never pitched an inning in his life! His left leg began to fold. He was going to fall—no—he would pretend to be tying his shoestring! He caught himself on his hands, flopped over on his seat, bowed his head. There! That and the ground steadied him. He felt better already. Now to get that cussed shoestring!

His head cleared rapidly. Shucks! Couldn't turn sissy now. Not with Dad up there in the stands. Dad would never get over it—not "Big Jim" Burnett, the greatest slugger and outfielder in Broadmoor College history. Dad would be proud of him yet. If not as a slugging outfielder, then as a pitcher.

Starting *now!*

Chapter 2

THE FATAL NINTH

As Bronc Burnett stepped onto the pitching slab and turned to look toward home plate, a chill ran up his spine. Gee—it was a long way! Home plate didn't look any bigger than a postage stamp. How'd they expect a fellow to put one over that, anyhow—much less, "play for the corners"?

His catcher was coming out to talk to him. Still half numbed by the sudden turn of things, Bronc didn't go to meet him. Just stood and waited.

The catcher was grinning through his mask. It was Fat Crompton!

"I'm familiar with what you've got," Fat explained, "so, Cap'n Al thought I'd better do the backstopping. How do you feel?"

"Fine!" Bronc mumbled.

"That's swell! Now, about signals: suppose we use—"

"No, no!" Bronc interrupted hastily. "We won't need any signals! I'll use my fast ball—we'll just blaze it past them!"

"Okay! Power to you!"

Fat turned and strode back toward home plate.

Signals! Bronc shuddered again at the thought. Signals were for old heads who mixed them up; for men who dared to risk curves and slow balls along with their fast ones. Not for unfortunates like him! He'd be doing mighty well just to locate the platter with a fast one!

Who was the hitter, anyhow? There—big ox—already shaking his war club! The fellow wore a frown blacker than the inside of a black cat. Going to knock it a country mile, is he? Well, if—

"Hey, Bronc! Look out, Bronc! To second—quick!"

Fat Crompton's warning came too late. By the time Bronc whirled, the Spur base runner was already three fourths of the way to second, and nobody was covering the bag.

"Not your fault in there, Bronc!" Chic Stahl yelled afterward. "I shoulda been there. Shoulda had him by a mile! Just went to sleep, I guess. All right, let's go to work on the batter!" The little second baseman reached down, grabbed up a handful of dirt, threw it aside, wiped his hands on his pants, and crouched waiting. "Make him hit to me, Bronc! I'll even it up for you. Make him hit to me!"

Bronc turned again to the batter. The burly slugger was still brandishing his war club in a way that threatened to bust the cover completely off the ball.

Then, suddenly:

"Come on out there, son! Let's go, boy!"

His father's booming voice! From far up in the stands!

No medicine yet concocted could have braced Bronc Burnett half so much. A sunny, confident grin broke clear across his square features. He tried momentarily to locate his father, then waved his gloved hand in the general direction.

Pandemonium promptly broke loose from the visitors' bench. Here was a pitcher who would *listen*! Spur went into a huddle. Meanwhile Bronc, unsuspecting, was already winding up. He pivoted easily, reached back, thrust his left leg high in the air, and cut loose. The ball sped like a rifle shot—straight across the heart of the plate.

"Strike one!"

Bronc's head whirled happily. Shucks! This pitching wasn't any chore at all. All a fellow had to do—

What's that? On third—who?

Bronc turned. Then for the first time it dawned on him that the runner had taken advantage of his slow windup and easily stolen third. The tying run on third now—a dusty, grinning youngster threatening, even, to steal home. That wasn't so good, with only one down. A long fly to the outfield, or a slow-hit grounder, would enable the runner to score. Jiminy! It's up to me now, almost by myself! Should have remembered that Spur runner, all right. Should have held him on second. But a fellow can't think of everything. Anyhow, he'd shoved strike number one past the batter. That bluffer wasn't nearly as tough as he wanted folks to think he was. Only two more, and the gent could go sit down, mumbling to himself!

Then a disquieting thought occurred to Bronc: Maybe the batter, having seen that his teammate was dashing for third, had purposely let the strike be called against him. Otherwise he would have risked fouling it, thereby causing the runner to be sent back after having the base practically stolen. Yeah, there was that chance. Nasty thought, too, because this fellow might be a slugger, after all. Better to—

"Who said you were a pitcher?" one of the visiting team members hooted suddenly from the side line. "Why, they wouldn't even let you carry water, if your old daddy wasn't president of the school board!"

Bronc stared in amazement. His father wasn't on the school board. Never had been! What did this insulting yip-yap mean, anyhow?

"Are the Burnetts still in the chicken-stealing business?" jeered another uniformed player.

The whole Spur team was near the side line now, hooting and squawling at Bronc, having learned that he would listen.

He promptly started toward them. "If you gents are looking for trouble, I'll—"

Umpire Sheriff Drinkwater yanked off his mask and strode out from behind the plate. He motioned to Bronc with the mask in terms that Bronc could not misunderstand. "Get on back there! This is a ball game—not a side show!"

Slowly Bronc began to grin. "Okay, Sheriff! Sorry, but I sorta lost my head."

Bronc's quick, short steps returned him to the mound.

"You're going to lose more than your head!" one Spur jockey yelled between cupped hands. "Of course, that's the thing you can spare best!"

"*Play ball!*" stormed the umpire.

Without winding up this time, Bronc suddenly whipped the ball toward his catcher. Again it was in the groove, a tiny pellet that streaked into Crompton's mitt with the speed of light.

"Strike two!"

Bronc threw a defiant glance at his tormentors over on the side line. What would they have to say about that?

They had plenty! Enough that once more the umpire had to prevent Bronc from paying them a call in person!

The boy, green and uncoached on how to act in the face of such a storm, nervously managed to fire another sizzler across the plate for "Strike three!" The batter had swung this time, but considerably after the ball had plunked into Crompton's mitt.

Two down now! A runner still on third. The tying run, but that didn't matter. Not the way this new phenomenon, Bronc Burnett, was rifling the pill across!

Fat Crompton came running out to pat him on the back. So did Chic Stahl from second, and "Trail" Drover from short. The crowd, too, gave him a tremendous hand. Innocently, Bronc raised his cap and waved. That promptly set the wolves loose on him again.

"Yoo-hoo, sweetheart!"

"Hey! Waving at the undertaker? You'd better be—he's gonna have a job, quick as Butch knocks this next one down your throat!"

Bronc glared, his teeth gritted, his jaw stuck out like a bulldog.

Then suddenly, from the Sonora side of the field:

"Come on out there, Rabbit Ears!" It was Fibate Jones's voice, using an old baseball term for a pitcher who pays too much attention to the crowd. "Save some of that energy for the batter!"

Bronc whirled like a cutting horse. "You keep out of this, Fibate! You keep score. I'll handle my end of the deal!"

"Yeah—you'll handle it, just like Spur wants you to!"

Stung to the quick, Bronc went tense as a cougar getting ready to spring. But once more the umpire's authoritative "Play ball!" brought him back into the game. He took a quick look at the dancing, darting, threatening runner on third, then with an awkward half windup started his throw.

Bronc's pitch, thrown from an unbalanced position, struck the Spur batsman on the fleshy part of his thigh.

"Take your base!"

A wild chorus from the visiting wolves greeted the announcement. "Look who's coming to bat now—just look! It's Slug Langenegger, greatest hitter in the conference . . . three home runs already this year, and four triples! Well, it's good-by now, Mr. Pitcher! See you again next year, maybe!"

Then, from the other side of the diamond:

"They're right, Burnett! This man is hitting five-eighty. You should have taken more pains with the other man. He couldn't hit the size of his hat! That was a boner! If you lose a ball game for Sonora—" Fibate Jones didn't get to finish the sentence.

Cap'n Al Carter's big hand had muffled the words at the source of origin. With his free hand he now motioned to Bronc. "Don't pay any attention, Burnett—not to anybody! Just go ahead and pitch ball!"

Bronc nodded. He wiped nervous sweat from his forehead with one sleeve, meanwhile studying the batter. He was big, all right. Big, limber, and ready. Bronc gritted his teeth. "Can't hit it, if he can't see it!" he muttered. He turned the ball loose with every bit of power in his rangy one-seventy.

Doggone it! He'd forgotten again about the runner—the runner on first. Or, rather, the one who had been on first. Now he was parked on second. Another clean steal. Runners on second and third—the tying and winning runs—and murderous Slug Langenegger at bat!

Nor was that all: "Ball one!" the umpire had judged Bronc's first pitch.

Fat Crompton came walking out toward him. Bronc went down to meet him. "How do you feel, pardner?"

"Fine!"

"Then let's try a curve on this gentleman. What do you say?"

"Okay by me."

Fat turned and hurried back to his post. Bronc stood watching the runners on second and third from the corner of his eye until his catcher was ready. Then he toed the slab.

"You'll wish you were back home in jail, by the time Slug gets through with you!" a Spur player jeered.

Bronc turned, angrily trying to see which player had hurled the insult. He'd never been in jail in his life, and it was "dirty pool" for this yip-yap to yell such a thing. If that was the way Spur—

"*Hey! Never mind! Play the batter!* They're just trying to rattle you on purpose. Play the batter!"

Bronc whirled, saw that it was Cap'n Al Carter from

the other side. He nodded obediently. "Sure, Coach! I sorta forgot." Once more he turned to face home plate and Slug Langenegger.

All right, let's see what the famed slugger will do to this one! This ol' fireball will be so fast it will make a rocket look slow!

Bronc started his delivery. Then, in horror, he remembered: Fat Crompton had wanted a curve—would be set for a curve! Too late now—the ball slipped as Bronc tried desperately to change.

"It's wild! A wild pitch! Come on! Come on in!"

The alert runner dashed across from third. The score was tied, nine to nine!

Bronc himself ran down toward the plate. "*Quick, Fat!*" he squalled out. "The man on second—he's going to third!"

Fat Crompton had retrieved the ball by this time, and now whirled about. He heaved an excited, aimless throw in the general direction of third, but it went high above the baseman's head into short left field. The second Spur runner scored easily, far in advance of little Peedink Harrell's weak throw to cut him off.

Spur leads—ten to nine!

When the hubbub finally subsided, an angry, bitter, vengeful Bronc Burnett took the slab once more. Two down. The bases clean. Now he'd show them! And he did! Slug Langenegger worked him for a walk, but three straight fireballs across the plate, smoking hot, humbled the next man in short order. The side retired. Last of the ninth coming up. Sonora now one run behind.

"Come on, gang! Let's get some runs. We can do it, gang! Come on now, everybody on their toes! Who's first batter? Who's on deck? Let's get that run back . . . let's get two. . . ."

The late evening sun was nearly set, with long shadows blanketing the field as Sonora readied for the final bats. The stands were still packed—now noisy, now hushed, now a bedlam again. Behind the plate, lanky Pole Drinkwater, county sheriff and umpire of the day, carefully put on his mask and signaled play.

Chic Stahl had flied out to center field for the windup of the preceding inning, so Buck Losey would be leading off. Buck, the quick-witted, nimble-footed little third baseman for Sonora, had only a .216 average for the season thus far, according to Fibate Jones's figures, but each of his hits had figured in the scoring. Good man in a pinch, all right. Come on, Buck! Paste the old apple down somebody's throat! Get on, Buck! Somebody will drive you in!

Buck Losey came through. He spanked the first pitch for a clean single into right. The crowd, sensing new hope, gave him delirious applause. Nobody away; their fastest, smartest runner on first. Why, he'd steal the pitcher's glove, if it wasn't screwed on. Just give Buck half a chance, he'd be across with the tying run.

Trail Drover was already at the plate. Trail, the team captain and shortstop, who had hit two singles already that day. Trail looked confident now. He was relaxed, swinging easily, the bill of his cap bent, and a part grin on his lips.

The first pitch was a ball, wide of the plate. The Spur catcher barely managed to shag it, and promptly fired it down to first, where Buck Losey slid back to base. Buck had taken a big lead, almost in the notion of breaking for second. The crowd held its breath until "Safe!" set them to chattering again.

The ball went back to the pitcher. Once more Buck Losey crept farther and farther from first. The pitcher eyed him doubtfully, decided against a throw, then whipped one across to the batter. Trail Drover hit it on the nose—a line smash that was still rising when it reached the pitcher—but the pitcher somehow managed

23

to leap into the air and snag it with one hand. Quickly he whirled, shot the ball to first.

Double play! Buck Losey had started for second, then was too late to recover and get back. A concerted groan escaped from the crowd. Should have been at least a two-bagger! "Base hit" labeled all over it! Just one inch higher—one inch—*anywhere else*, and instead of a double play Buck Losey would now be across the pan with a run! Tough break, all right. The sacks empty again, and two away.

Who's the next batter? Red Bailey, right fielder. Bronc Burnett on deck. Little Peedink Harrell in the hole.

Red didn't waste any time. With the visiting pitcher showing obvious signs of fatigue, he smashed a mighty triple between left and center. It would have been a home run for some of the other boys, but the slower-running Bailey was held up at third.

Again the crowd took hope. It was several minutes before the stands subsided, and even then, everybody remained on his feet. Two away, but the tying run was in easy scoring position. Another hit, or even an error by the Spur team, which now showed signs of tension, would do the business. Come on, Burnett! Win your own game, boy! Redeem yourself, boy!

Bronc stepped grimly into the box, pounded his bat on the plate, then looked at the opposing pitcher.

Oh, brother! What wouldn't he give for a home run! That would show Dad. Would show everybody—except, maybe, that little gadfly, Fibate Jones! The Spur pitcher looked tired, all right. Tired and worried, both. Bronc almost felt sorry for him—but this pitcher would just have to take it.

"Ten times at bat without a hit!" he heard Fibate yell from the bench. "But come home, son, all is forgiven, if you'll only get one now!"

Bronc glanced back over his shoulder. If that little gadfly didn't—

Too late, Bronc saw the pitch coming.

"Strike one!" the umpire announced.

"But I wasn't ready!"

Pole Drinkwater shook his head. "You were in the box, in position," he said. "I'm sorry, but it's still strike one!"

Bronc bit his lip. Oh, well, that was only one. Still two big ones left. Only takes one to hit it, anyhow. I'm not in any hole at all—that pitcher just thinks I am. He'll probably try to sneak a curve across the outside now. Figures I've got my dauber down, after losing that first strike. Yeah, he figures I'll bite at anything. But I won't! It's got to be in there. And if it is, I'm going to slug from the heels. A home run, maybe, but no biting. If he tries to tempt me with an outside curve, I'll just let 'er go, then he'll have to shovel the next one across. Okay now, boy! Steady—here she comes—headed for the outside corner, all right! I'll just let 'er break off into the dirt.

But the ball didn't break.

"Strike two!" the umpire called it.

Hot blood crimsoned Bronc's face. Doggone it, that wasn't any way to play ball! What kind of pitching was that? Get a batter in the hole and then groove one! Plenty lucky out there, Mr. Pitcher! You sure had a rabbit's foot tied to that one. If you hadn't, I'd have slapped it right on the nose!

All right, where do we stand now? Two and nothing! Aw, that ain't so bad as it sounds. You'll have to waste a couple now, probably outside with the first one, then one in close to my brisket—that's just fundamental baseball. You've got 'em to spare, and you figure I haven't. You figure I might be tempted by a bad one. Then, even if I hit it, it wouldn't go far. But I'm not tumbling for any such bait, Mr. Pitcher! It's gotta be in there, even if the count is two and nothing against me. So go ahead and try to bait me—yeah, just try it! I'm ready to—

"Steady in there, Pitch . . . don't lose him. . . ." the Spur infield chattered to their hurler. "Easy man! Let's play the easy man! Don't take any chances. . . . Peedink Harrell comes up next! Let's play for this easy man. . . ."

Bronc swallowed hard. But he had learned his lesson about taking his eyes off the man on the mound, and so managed to fight down his impulse to single out the exact speakers in the opposing line-up.

All right, come on, Mr. Pitcher! Let's hurry with this pair of waste balls, and get down to business. Then it will be either you or me, Mr. Pitcher—one of us will be a goat, and the other a hero! Jiminy! I hope Daddy didn't raise any goats—only ballplayers! I'll show him. I've got to! Quick as these two waste balls are a thing of the past, I'll sock. Here comes number one!

Bronc watched it calmly, confidently.

Oh, for gosh sakes! That dumbbell pitcher had grooved a fat one! Grooved it—on a two-and-nothing count!

Then the four most terrifying words in the English language: "Strike three—you're out!"

That was the longest, blackest night of Bronc Burnett's young life. To begin with, he avoided the school bus, with its inevitable load of chattering, jeering students, and walked home. Seven miles. Three up the winding, climbing trail to the summit, then four more down the other side of the shadowy, timber-darkened range to the Burnett ranch in Lobo Valley.

There was a light in the front room, and he could see that they were already preparing for bed, so he didn't go inside. He'd wait—give Dad and Mother time to get to sleep.

"Gosh!" he muttered, with a mirthless grin. "Didn't

26

the whole world fall on top of me today? I'm lucky to still be alive!"

He'd probably miss seeing his father in the morning, though. Maybe just as well, after the way he'd let his dad down.

"He'll be gone by daylight, and Mom will let me sleep late in the morning," Bronc decided, while shivering outside in the darkness. "That way I won't have to answer any questions!"

Bronc's reasoning was considerably better than it had been against the Spur pitcher.

He did manage to slip into bed unobserved, and after two or three hours of restless tossing, dropped off to sleep. It was midmorning when big hands roughly awakened him. He blinked dazedly.

"Fat! What—what're you doing here this time of night?"

Fat Crompton made no reply. Stepping around the end of the bed, he threw up the window shade, letting brilliant sunlight flood the room.

Bronc raised himself sleepily. He yawned, stretched both arms high above his head, then settled a bleary-eyed gaze on his companion. Something in Fat's expression, however, immediately roused him.

"What's the matter? Somebody's funeral?"

"Maybe—yours and mine!" Fat Crompton tossed a small newspaper onto the bed. "Read that!"

Bronc picked up the paper, the Sonora weekly *Messenger*, advertised as being published every Thursday but invariably one or two days late. Quickly he glanced at the heads. There, about halfway down, right-hand column:

"SONORA DROPS THRILLER IN NINTH"

He read on:

"For eight and one third innings here this afternoon, Al Carter's scrappy little high school nine had visiting

27

Spur practically beaten and buried, but at that point a savage line drive split the fingers of 'Pitch' Carson's business hand and his successor, Sophomore Bronc Burnett, simply couldn't hold the dyke.

"Burnett might not have fared so badly, at that, if he hadn't developed an extremely sensitive pair of rabbit ears, which caused him to pay more attention to the crowd than to the game. As a result, he wild-pitched the contest into a predicament that not even a budding rally in the home ninth was able to remedy."

There followed more of the early inning details, a bouquet for little Peedink Harrell, and the box score.

"Well, what do you think of that?"

"Not bad," Bronc said. "I was expecting a lot worse. After all, I did singlehandedly lose us a ball game. It looks to me as if the editor—"

"The editor? I didn't mean him! Look at Fibate's column! There—under the high school notes! That's what I'm hollering about!"

Bronc followed Fat's thick finger to a smaller, boxed column at the bottom center:

"The Spur *eleven* won over our Sonora high school *seven* here this afternoon by a score of ten to nine. Outstanding for the invaders was the work of Bronc Burnett and Arthur (Fat) Crompton, who although disguised in the uniform of the home team, actually provided the winning margin for their buddies from down in the valley.

"It is devoutly to be hoped that neither of these fifth columnists will ever again get a chance to infiltrate and undermine our line-up. On your guard, Cap'n Al!"

Bronc's powerful young body went stiff, his steel-gray eyes narrow, as throbbing arteries began to stand out on his temples. Presently he turned to his companion. "What're *you* aiming to do about it? Decided yet?"

Fat nodded. "It wasn't hard for me to decide. And I'm not changing my mind. But let's hear yours first."

Bronc Burnett slid his trim, wide-shouldered body on-to the side of the bed, reaching for his slippers. "Did you bring your mitt along?" he asked.

His companion began to grin. "Yeah."

"Good! It seems we're agreed. The way to make him eat those words is on the diamond. I'll be ready in ten minutes, and we'll practice all day!"

Chapter 3

SKULL PRACTICE

Bronc Burnett was ready for the world by Monday morning. Expecting the worst, dreading it, of course, but determined to take it with a grin.

"Gotta keep a halter on my temper," he told himself. "After all, I did lose a ball game for the gang. Bumped us out of first place. So, they've got a right to pull my tail feathers if they want to!"

Bronc passed his first test with honors. It had come the instant he boarded the school bus.

"Howdy, Rabbit Ears!" called Chic Stahl, the team's hustling little second baseman, who lived on the neighboring "Flying H" Ranch. "How's the ol' slugger this morning?" But Chic accompanied the words with a broad grin.

"Fine!" Bronc responded. "Cocky enough to ride a tornado without a bridle!"

The seat beside Stahl was occupied, so Bronc gave him a friendly squeeze on the shoulder as he passed, and went on to the back of the bus. He dropped down beside a ten-year-old, who watched him from the corner of his eye for a moment, then ventured:

"Gee! If you could only play ball like your father used to, why, I betcha we'd have won that game Friday."

"Stick around, sonny! There'll be more games."

The bus was several minutes behind its regular sched-

ule that morning, and it was practically nine o'clock before the students reached school. On his way to physics,
first class, Bronc almost bumped into Fibate Jones at the
head of the main stairway. Fibate and "Wasp" Dillon,
another bookish youngster of about the same age, were
also headed for the physics class.

Bronc hesitated only momentarily. He began to grin.
"Howdy, Fibate! All set for a quiz this morning?"

Fibate stared blankly. Then with well-pretended dig-
nity, he adjusted his glasses and shoved his thin, sharp
face several inches closer to Bronc. "Your voice seems to
be familiar," he murmured. "And your face—where
could I have seen that face before?"

"What do you mean?"

"Now I remember: you were at the ball game last Friday—dressed up in a suit just like the other Sonora
players. Only, you didn't play for Sonora!"

Wasp Dillon giggled through one hand.

"There'll be more games," Bronc said stiffly. "You
gents stick around!" He shoved Fibate aside and strode
into the classroom without a word to anybody else. He
took his seat, eyes straight ahead. The bell rang.

The class proceeded routinely through a brief résumé
of the work covered during the week before, then the
instructor announced a ten-minute oral quiz on the assignment for that day.

"Mr. Jones," he said, indicating Fibate, "suppose you
were occupying a room in which a Fahrenheit thermometer stood at thirty-two degrees. What would be the
comparable registration on a centigrade thermometer?"

"Bronc Burnett's hitting average!" Fibate mumbled,
without moving his lips, but loud enough for a dozen of
his classmates to hear.

A chorus of muffled snickers swept the circle about
him. Bronc, too, had heard, but he didn't snicker!

"What was that figure, Mr. Jones?"

"Zero, sir!" Fibate replied this time.

31

"Quite right."

That little coyote—why hadn't somebody drowned him when he was a pup? Why couldn't the rest of them have been drowned, too—snickering like that, at something that wasn't even halfway funny! So these were his classmates, huh? *Classmates!* The word was a mockery. Maybe it was a good thing, after all, that they'd lost a game last Friday. Served 'em right. They didn't deserve to win; not a pack of coyotes like these, yip-yapping along behind a mongrel leader. As far as he was concerned, their old ball team could—

Wait a minute there, Bronc!

As if prodded with the business end of a spur, Bronc Burnett suddenly got hold of himself. What was this rubbish he had been thinking, anyhow? Got to do better than that! They can't rile me. They *can't*, because I won't let them. No, sir! It's like Dad says: a ballplayer is a man with guts and a glove!

"In that event," droned the instructor's voice, "what would be the equivalent in loss of weight, Mr. Burnett?"

Bronc started. "I'm sorry, sir! Would you please repeat the question?"

There was a moment's tense silence. Then:

"It seems, Mr. Burnett, that you are most adept at sleeping—whether it be in class, or in the ninth inning of an important ball game!"

This time it was more than snickers that greeted Bronc's discomfiture. The class laughed openly. But Bronc had whipped his trouble, for the time being, at least, and although his big hands (under the desk, where they didn't show) knotted themselves into powerful fists, he managed to produce a wry grin, which he turned to display briefly for his classmates.

"I'm sorry, sir! If you'll give me another pitch, I'll swing on this one—sure!"

The period dragged endlessly for the uncomfortable youngster, and he could have shouted in relief when the bell finally did ring. He was the first student into the hallway, gulped a quick swallow of water, and then wiped moisture from his forehead, which had been caused far more by nervous strain than classroom heat.

The ten o'clock class in Spanish was much better. Bronc purposely delayed entering the room until time for the lesson actually to begin, and not even his so-called rabbit ears could detect any personal comment from the other students as he quietly took his seat. Probably because Fibate Jones was elsewhere!

The only reference to baseball was a scrawled notice on the blackboard that practice would begin thirty minutes earlier today. At two instead of two-thirty, and for some reason it had been scheduled for a classroom on the basement floor rather than the practice diamond outside.

Promptly at two, Cap'n Al Carter entered the room. The buzz of careless talk hushed instantly, as twenty sets of eager, admiring young eyes swung to the former big leaguer. Cap'n Al hadn't played professional ball for some ten years, but like all former players could never separate himself entirely from the game. He had come west to Sonora the preceding fall on account of his wife's health. Not only had she done well from the start, but they had both loved the verdant, pine-clad forest and the crisp, high-country air. The purchase of a small ranch had followed. Then, inevitably, the offer to help these high school boys when they lost their coach, with the baseball season just beginning.

Cap'n Al's big shoulders and long arms were very much in evidence, though clothed in a loose-fitting sweat shirt, as he shut the door and stepped lightly to the front of the room.

"Everybody on time?"

"Everybody was ten minutes early!" Fibate Jones responded promptly. "That's what we think of our new skipper!"

The coach merely grunted, though a pleased expression did soften the corners of his mouth. Seating himself on a corner of the desk, one leg dangling, the other propped stiffly against the floor, he studied the eager-faced group for a moment.

"Out there on the diamond," he said presently, "when a man makes an error he should forget it immediately. Not brood about it. But this is nearly three days later now, and we can go back over things quietly. No chance of a hot one smacking us in the belly, or the umpire calling a strike while we're busy thinking—

"Never mind!" he snapped abruptly, as two or three of the youngsters stole side glances toward the reddening Bronc Burnett. "I didn't have anybody particularly in mind; just doing some generalizing."

He paused. There wasn't a sound in the hushed room for several seconds, until the coach began speaking again.

"The first thing I want to say is that you looked awful out there Friday. It made me ashamed—being responsible for a lazy, shiftless aggregation as you were, against Spur. Now, hold on!" he cautioned hastily, as the young faces showed increasing tension. "I know you *thought* you were hustling—you kept up a chatter—you threw the old pill around—you trotted back and forth onto the diamond.

"But, gentlemen, that isn't enough. From now on, you're going to continue to do all those things, just as you did, but you're going to do a lot more. All right, you wonder: What does this guy mean? Well, I'll tell you!"

Suddenly Cap'n Al shot a finger at little Peedink Harrell.

"We'll start with you! And don't any of the rest of you think your own turn isn't coming, either. You all needed a good, strong boot toe applied to the seat of your pants! But as for you, Peedink: there in the first of the ninth, two down, as a runner scored from third on Burnett's wild pitch, you acted like a cash customer in-

34

stead of a player! None of your affair, you probably thought. You hadn't made the wild pitch—you hadn't failed to catch it. Somebody else's bust! Meanwhile, the runner on second took third. You watched that, too. Still, none of your affair—what the heck—you were only the left fielder! But—"

Cap'n Al Carter banged the desk so savagely, so unexpectedly, that every boy in the room jumped.

"From now on," he snapped, "you'll be running till your tongue hangs out to back up the bases on plays like that. It doesn't even matter whether there's actually a throw, or not. If there's even a chance there *might* be a throw, you'll be on the move, always assuming the worst. Always preparing, in advance, for the worst. Get the idea? You'll have a lot to do there in left, the same as you other gardeners: you in center, and you in right!" Cap'n Al followed the words with a motion, indicating Bill Burnham and Red Bailey.

"Any time there's a play for a base, or as I just said, even the *chance* of a play for a base, I want you to pretend the ball is going to be missed. Nine times out of ten you won't be needed. But on the tenth—well—it would have kept us in the ball game last Friday if Peedink had been there to intercept Crompton's bad throw to third. The runner could have been held there. Instead, he scored.

"Now, don't any of you yahoots get the idea I am suggesting, or even implying, that Peedink Harrell singlehandedly lost the game for us Friday. As a matter of fact, he probably helped more than anybody else, save possibly Pitch Carson, to keep us in the running until the final inning. But it just goes to show that baseball is played by a team—a team of nine men—practically all of the time. Of course, with nobody down, it frequently narrows the battle ground to home plate. Batter versus pitcher. But even then, there's still a job for every man on both teams all of the time.

"Let's look at it as the defensive team first. Remember the situation now: nobody on base. As a casual observer would think, just a two-man affair; the batter is trying to get on, the pitcher is trying to prevent.

"In a situation like this, most of you would figure the defensive team has nothing to do but watch and wait. But that's the wrong attitude. It isn't hustling, as you're going to hustle for me!

"The instant the batter stepped to the plate, for example, every single one of you should have studied him. Was he grinning, or tense? Did he look anxious and eager to hit, or a little hesitant? How about his stance? Got a long grip on the bat as if he wants to kill one, or is he choking up short for a place hit? And what did he do on previous tries . . . fan, fly to the outfield, draw a base on balls, or single to right field? And where does he bat in the line-up?

"What difference would that make, Stahl?" he asked abruptly.

But before Chic could answer, the coach resumed: "If a man is hitting either first or second, then he's apt to be cagey and smart, a good waiter, and a fast man on his feet. If he's down in third, fourth, or fifth place, he's one of their three best hitters; if third, particularly, their surest hitter, if fourth, their longest hitter, and so forth. All of these things determine how deep a team should play. Not only the outfield, but the infield, too. The deeper an infield can play, the more ground they can cover. But for one of those two lead-off men—the smart, fast little men—an infield wouldn't dare play too deep. Wouldn't have time to throw 'em out on ground balls. But on a big slugger, batting in fourth place, it's usually safe to play back. Why, Drover?"

"Because we'd have an extra second of time on the play at first," the team captain replied promptly.

"Right! Now for something I hinted at a moment before: What did he do on previous tries? That's what we call playing 'percentage ball.' In the big leagues it is worked out to a science, because the teams play over a hundred fifty games a year, and each regular bats four or five times per game. So when a batter comes up, for example, we have in the back of our mind the fact that he has batted, let us say, one hundred times already that season. He has got, say, thirty-two hits. Of these, twenty-eight have been singles, three doubles, and one triple—not a long hitter, but a fairly good one. So let's narrow it down even further: of those thirty-two hits, twenty-four have been to right field, seven to center, and only one to left. Okay, Mr. Batter, we're ready for you! There's an overwhelming percentage of your knocking a single to right field, if you hit it safely. So we immediately shift our men around and cluster them where the base hit is most apt to fall.

"If our pitcher starts curving him, we'll ease back a trifle toward normal position. The batter would be swinging a little fast. If it's to be fast-ball pitching, we'll move even farther to the right, changing with each pitched ball. That is," Cap'n Al corrected himself, "if we're pitching to right-handed batters. It'll be just the reverse, of course, for the lefties.

"There are dozens more of these things that an alert, hustling outfielder must keep in his head. I'm not going into too much detail this early, because I don't want to confuse you, but I do want to knock into your heads—for all time to come—that a man is part of the team *all of the time*, not merely when a play comes toward him.

"It's the same with the team on offense. A good ballplayer doesn't sit there on the bench, lazy and indifferent, until it's his turn to bat or run. All of that time he's using his eyes and his head, and talking baseball with the guys sitting next to him. Somebody notices that the pitcher is consistently throwing a fast ball, right through the groove, on the first pitch to each batter. Okay, we'll be ready for it! Another notices that he always uses a

37

curve on a one-and-one count. Okay, just let him try to pull that on me! And with an inexperienced, or tense pitcher, you can almost always count on a fast one, with all the smoke he's got for the 'three-two' pitch. It takes nerve and confidence to throw a curve or a slow one at a time like that, but if a man can do it, he'll probably win. But let's get back to the bench:

"Somebody else has noticed that the pitcher isn't breaking for first on balls hit to his left. Okay, as soon as we get a good bunter to the plate, we'll try laying one down fairly deep toward first. If the first baseman comes running in to field it, we'll have a good chance of beating him to the bag, because the pitcher has unconsciously been indicating that he will be too slow to cover. This, of course, depends on the ability of our batter to run speedily, as well as bunt; and it depends, too, on the position and nature of the rival second baseman, because some of them, when playing close, always cover first for slow pitchers.

"So, you see, there's a lot to be watching while we wait for our turn to hit. And this watching and scheming and off-time planning are all part of what I mean by 'hustle.' You're going to be a hustling team. You're either going to hustle, or—well—you're either going to hustle, or I'll break your doggone backs!" But the coach's broad grin belied some of the savagery in his words.

"We'll take up the various positions individually," he concluded, "after we get out on the practice field. Also, some more of the faults you yahoots committed last Friday. The main thing I want you to understand now, thoroughly, is that you're to be a hustling team. Three men on every ball!

"Any questions, so far?"

There was a moment of silence, while the twenty pairs of eager eyes remained fixed on their idol. Then:

"What are we going to do for pitchers?" Fibate Jones

blurted significantly. "We've got two games this week —Lakewood on Wednesday, and Hope on Friday—and Doc Esberg says that Pitch Carson, here, won't be able to throw for at least ten days on account of his busted finger. With Lefty Lear and Red Bailey as the only other possibilities, what are we going to do?"

Bronce Burnett felt every muscle in his body go tense at Fibate's indirect cut, but he did not look around. Just kept his eyes glued on Cap'n Al.

The coach's strong face revealed a momentary frown, then he nodded pleasantly to Fibate. "Thanks for the question! It reminds me of something I had nearly forgotten. Take this piece of chalk and copy our standings on the board—percentages and all. Then we'll do a little more skull practice before going outside."

He tossed the chalk to Fibate, who was already out of his seat and starting to the blackboard.

"I don't need my notebook!" Fibate said proudly.

"Fine!"

"Shall I write off our schedule too?"

"Excellent idea!"

"I don't need my notebook for that either!"

Fibate wrote rapidly, then stepped aside so the team could see. Cap'n Al, too, surveyed it interestedly. The standings of the Sapello Valley conference were:

Position	Teams	Won	Lost	Percentage
1.	Spur	3	0	1.000
2.	Greenfield	3	0	1.000
3.	Sonora	2	1	.667
4.	Suerte	2	1	.667
5.	Tatum	2	1	.667
6.	Hope	1	2	.333
7.	Concho	1	2	.333
8.	Mesquite	1	2	.333
9.	Vocant	0	3	.000
10.	Lakewood	0	3	.000

The schedule called for nine games, with each of the ten teams playing one game with each of the other conference members.

"We won't dig up any more past history," Cap'n Al said, "by crying over spilt milk. You can see where we'd be now, if last Friday's game had turned out otherwise, but that's all past. It's the future that concerns us. For instance: Spur and Greenfield play one another Wednesday. Get the idea? One of them will drop down. Then we'll be tied for second place, if we beat Lakewood. That will be a notch higher up. And if Greenfield beats Spur, which isn't unlikely, as they will be playing in Greenfield, that becomes a good break for us."

"What's the difference?" Peedink Harrell wanted to know. "Won't the percentage be the same, a four and nothing, for either Spur or Greenfield—whichever wins?"

"The same—yes. But with Greenfield on top, we'll have a chance to play them. We're through with Spur. See?"

"Oh, boy! Here's a new fan for Greenfield!"

Other members chimed in enthusiastically, but a quick gesture from Cap'n Al cut them short.

"It all adds up to one thing," he reminded them soberly. "We've got to beat Lakewood on Wednesday as a starter."

The boys swapped glances.

Beat Lakewood? Shucks, they're a push-over! Why, they're floundering clear down at the bottom of the pile! Lost twenty to three last week to Concho, and we beat Concho nine to one. Gee—it'll be murder!

"Who's going to pitch for us?" Fibate wanted to know, as the room quieted momentarily.

"Can't say—yet. It wouldn't be fair to Red Bailey or Lefty Lear, whom I haven't seen in action. But you can

40

put this into your thinking cap: I've still got a lot of hope tied up in Bronc Burnett."

Whew! Did you hear that, Fibate? Did you hear it, you razor-tongued little smart aleck?

Bronc left the room, his head in a dizzy whirl. Somebody clutched him by the arm, then linked elbows with him. It was Fat Crompton, grinning from one ear to the other. Together they did an old-fashioned schottische down the corridor and out onto the field.

There was no doubt about who was boss of the Sonora high school team, once they reached the diamond. Within seconds' time, almost, the fiery ex-leaguer had them paired off to limber up for their first practice under his guidance.

He allowed ten minutes. Then, with half the squad rushed onto the field to shag balls, he started hitting practice. And while the hitters awaited their turns, he kept them busy in a strenuous, peppery high-low game along the third-base line. Along first, he had Lefty Lear and Red Bailey warming up with the team's regular catcher, Drake Yoder. Nobody loafed. Everybody hustled.

"Burnett," the coach had ordered, "whenever your arm is ready, you throw to the hitters."

"It's ready now, sir."

"Are you sure? Don't want to take any chances."

"It never felt better in my life!"

"Okay! But take it easy for a few throws. You'll get more than you want before the afternoon is over, anyhow. Now, no curves, mind you. Just plain, straight stuff, just as near the center as you can groove them. This is batting practice, not pitching practice. Understand?"

"Yes, sir!"

"Good! Crompton, you get behind the plate," Cap'n Al ordered next. "Give him a target on every pitch. It's hard work, but it will help him. As for you, it'll be a good thing to work some of that lard off, anyhow!" Again the coach's disarming grin took all the sting from his words.

Fat Crompton trotted over to his assignment, as eager as a collie pup with a new toy.

The coach presently waylaid Smitty when the big first baseman had finished taking his cuts at the ball. "I've got a quarrel with you," he announced.

"Me? Gosh! What have I done?"

"The little matter of losing us a ball game last Friday."

"Me? Gosh, Cap'n Al! I got three for five at the plate. That's hitting a cool six hundred. And nine chances at first without an error. What does a man have to do, if—"

"On three different occasions," the coach interrupted quietly, "you let throws pull you off the base to your right; throws that were in plenty of time to get the runner, if your foot had been on the base."

"But that was the thrower's fault!" Smitty protested.

"Partly, yes. But the three times I'm talking about, it happened because you had your footwork wrong. Now, I'll concede that some very good first basemen habitually kick the bag, always with the same foot. But they're exceptions, and on plays to their weak side they have to catch the ball backhanded. New players shouldn't learn that way; gets them cross-legged.

"Here's the way you'll do it for me: When you reach to the right for a ball—like this, see?—you should touch the bag with your left foot. Vice versa, when you stretch to the left to take a throw, you tag with your right. Gives you nearly twelve inches more reach—enough that we would have caught those three runners out easy last Friday. Instead, they were on. Later, two of them scored."

"Gosh!" Smitty muttered, thoroughly chastened now.

"I never knew that before. It won't happen again, Coach!"

"Yes, it probably will, for a while. It's a tricky move and has to become instinctive. But I want you to practice the shift. Try it a hundred times! Then you'll be able to do it correctly without thinking, and it will save us two or three outs, ordinarily, in every game. That's an edge we can't spare."

One at a time, Cap'n Al called the other regulars similarly aside. Expertly and convincingly he showed them that each man had lost the ball game! Some little slip, or in some cases several slips, had contributed to a Spur run, or had cost Sonora one. It was unbelievable. Yet, when explained by Cap'n Al, there it was. A fellow just *had* to believe it!

The conclusion: inevitable, of course, that baseball was a team game from the first "Play ball!" to the last "You're out!"

Bronc Burnett did well that afternoon. The more he threw, the more his confidence returned, especially as Cap'n Al had time to coach him on his delivery.

"We'll work on your throws to bases tomorrow," Carter promised. "It is extremely important to make runners hug the sacks. Prevents them from stealing a base, perhaps into scoring position, besides holding down their lead in case the batter connects. Tomorrow I'll show you the stance, how to pivot, and which way to snap a throw to each base. They're all different."

Bronc beamed his thanks, too happy to put them into words. But there was more yet to his day of triumph, from a most unexpected source.

Shortly before time to call a halt to the day's work, Cap'n Al motioned them to assemble. They were a sweaty, puffing, tired bunch—and Fat Crompton was practically out on his feet—but there wasn't a dull set of eyes in the lot, or a boy who was ready to quit. A

43

serious-faced man, perhaps in his early forties, wearing gray pants, without a coat, and a small, "city-style" brown hat, hurried out to stand beside Cap'n Al.

"Boys, there's no need to introduce our guest. You all know him, better than I do. So I'll simply say that Mr. Harold Dye, editor of the *Sonora Messenger*, wants to say a few words. Okay, Mr. Dye, you're on deck!"

"Thank you, Al!" The editor cleared his throat, glanced briefly at the circle of curious faces. "Fellows," he said, then, "I have come here in all humility to apologize. A most unfortunate item slipped past me in our hurry to publish last week's paper."

He paused, clearing his throat again.

"I am referring, of course, to the 'School Notes' column written by Fibate Jones, and to the very derogatory remarks concerning Bronc Burnett that appeared therein. I deeply regret—"

"Did you see the game, Mr. Dye?" Fibate broke in angrily. "Did you see how Bronc and Fat deliberately tossed away our victory?"

"Why, you little wart!" Bronc snarled. "Deliberately, did you say? I'll—" He started toward Fibate.

But the editor, with surprising agility, stepped between them. He faced Bronc squarely, holding out his hand.

"I saw the game, Burnett," he said. "But that doesn't make the slightest bit of difference, one way or another. The write-up shouldn't have appeared, and I sincerely want to apologize."

Bronc took the proffered hand with some embarrassment. "Aw, shucks! It really did me good. Fat and I practiced nearly all the next day. But thanks, Mr. Dye!"

Sudden, spontaneous clapping broke from the group. Fibate Jones crimsoned, but only for an instant. And obviously sensing the way the tide was running, he took immediate action.

44

"I'm sorry, too, Bronc!" he said. "Will you shake with me?"

"Sure!"

On the way to the showers, after Cap'n Al had sent them all running two laps around the bases, Fat Crompton staggered exhaustedly over beside his buddy. "Want —to—know—something?" he panted, laying a heavy hand on Bronc's shoulder.

"Fire away!"

"You're—you're going to pitch the game Wednesday!"

"How do you know?"

"I heard Fibate arguing in favor of Lefty Lear, but Cap'n Al—well, Cap'n Al shut him up mighty quick. You're going to have to keep an eye on Fibate, pardner —he's a smooth one. That handshake was just a grandstand play. Actually, he's— What the heck?" snorted Crompton. "I don't believe you heard a word I said!"

Bronc chuckled delightedly. "I heard what counted most!" he replied. "So I'm to start against Lakewood? Jiminy! I've got to get word to Dad, somehow!"

"What about Fibate?"

"Oh, he's an incurable disease. I'll just have to suffer along with him. A fellow just can't hit a weakling like him—he'd break all to pieces."

"But why does he needle *you* so much? He's always a chronic wise guy, I know, but it seems like he spews more poison at you than all the rest of us put together."

"Probably because the little coyote has learned that his yipping bothers me. And he's also learned that I won't bloody his nose. So he's just got worse and worse. But the heck with Fibate. I'm going to start on the mound against Lakewood! That's what really counts— gee!"

Bronc never remembered climbing the steps, or taking a shower afterward. His mind was already miles

45

away—across the mountain with his father. Dad would be happy now. At *last!*

He could beat Lakewood, all right. Sure he could, with this hustling team behind him. As for his rabbit ears, that was kid stuff. He'd learned his lesson well. They would never bother him again. Just let 'em try it! He hoped they would; that way, they wouldn't be bothering his teammates. Sure, just let 'em try it.

Chapter 4

STARTING PITCHER

SHORTLY after the noonday bell had rung on the day of the game with Lakewood, a slim, blue-eyed girl came hurrying to Bronc Burnett in the noisy hallway. She was Marie Lucky, student secretary to the high school principal.

"You're wanted on the phone, Bronc," she said. "In Mr. Slayter's office."

"Thanks, Marie!"

Bronc followed her into the office and picked up the receiver.

"Hello! . . . Who? . . . Oh, Dad! Say, what brings you in? Hope nothing's wrong! . . . Oh, then you *did* get in to see the game. That's swell! . . . What's that? . . . Sure, I'll be right down. Anywhere you say. . . ."

He quit the building three steps at a time. His fast walk carried him rapidly through the one-streeted canyon town to a small restaurant, on the north side of the street.

A big man, both wide and deep of shoulder, and an even six feet in height, grinned from under a broad-brimmed beaver hat as Bronc entered the doorway. "Howdy, son! Hungry? Let's see what they've got!" Big Jim Burnett clamped Bronc on the shoulder with a paw that would nearly have covered first base, steering him to a table in one corner. "How about a steak?"

Reluctantly, Bronc shook his head. "Better not. Cap'n Al says we can have the works tonight, but to go easy this noon."

"That's right! Good advice. Then how about a sandwich and a glass of milk, and maybe some ice cream?"

"Fine!"

Mr. Burnett placed the order, then with both big hands clasped on the table in front of him, he leaned forward toward his son. "How's the new coach doing?"

"Fine, Dad! We're the luckiest batch of guys that ever wore spikes. He's taught us enough already to fill forty books. And he hasn't half started!"

"You mean, coaching on your hitting?"

"We haven't got around to my hitting yet," Bronc said hastily. "You see, he's been concentrating on my delivery. In throwing to the plate, I've been kicking my left foot too high with runners on base; doing it to give me extra speed, but at the same time it's been allowing the runners to steal."

A slight frown narrowed the pleasant face of Big Jim Burnett. He ran his huge fingers up through his black, well-groomed hair, then down to loosen the collar of his gray and black checkered shirt.

"You mean, he's trying to make a pitcher out of you?"

"Yes, sir—probably."

Mr. Burnett took a swallow of water, replaced the glass on the table, and continued to fondle it thoughtfully. "Probably just until your regular pitcher gets over his injury," he surmised. "Then you'll be back in the outer garden again."

Bronc surveyed his father intently. "You'd lots rather see me play the outfield than pitch?"

"Why, sure! Wouldn't you?"

"I'm not so sure, Dad. There's an awful lot to this pitching business. And you know what they say: Pitching is seventy-five per cent of a team's strength."

"So I've heard! They've been saying that ever since

I was in college. But pitchers don't win games. Their only job is on the defensive! It's the hitters who pound in the runs. That's what counts—which team gets the runs."

"But it's the pitcher, usually, who keeps the other team from getting as many runs as you! In other words, if I should pitch a shutout against Lakewood this afternoon, Sonora would only need one run to win. Isn't that right?"

"Exactly!" the older man instantly agreed. "Just what I've been saying: in order to win, you must get runs. And how are runs manufactured? By base hits, my boy!" Then Big Jim's mood changed abruptly. The familiar twinkle returned again to his steel-gray eyes, which were so much like his son's. "Suppose we compromise," he suggested. "If you bat in the winning run this afternoon, besides holding Lakewood in check from the mound, then we'll both prove our arguments!"

"It's a deal, Dad!"

At that point a waiter brought their lunch. Presently, when they had begun to eat, Big Jim grinned across at his son.

"Don't pay too much attention to my ranting," he said. "After all, I'm prejudiced, and I know it. I played the outfield. Never even tried anywhere else. So, just keep this in mind, son: No matter what position you play, or how you play it, I'm going to be up there in the stands pulling for you."

Bronc returned the grin gratefully.

"What time does the game start?" the big rancher inquired, when they had finished the meal.

"At three-thirty. And Cap'n Al says three-thirty means exactly that."

"Very good, too, I'd say! And now you'd better be running along. Don't you have a one o'clock class?"

"Yes, sir—in history." Bronc rose to his trim, lithe-muscled six feet. "I probably won't see you again till after the game. But don't worry, Dad. I'm set for them today. You can nudge the guy next to you and say: 'That's *my* kid out there pitching!' I won't let you be ashamed of me again."

"Good! Then I'll be expecting you to clout a whole flock of extra base hits!"

"So long, Dad! Here's hoping!"

Bronc waved good-by and hurried outside.

"The old buzzard!" he chuckled to himself. "His whole attitude on baseball is confined to one four-lettered word: *Swat!* Well, maybe I can swat a little for him today. Gee! Wouldn't he be pleased!"

Cap'n Al had his youthful protégés on the field an hour and a quarter before game time. They might have been a group of colts—prancing, running, jumping—thoroughly instilled with "hustle," and, seemingly, just the right proportion of confidence mixed with their hustle.

After the customary few minutes of warming up, Cap'n Al put them through a fast-moving hitting practice, with Red Bailey pouring them straight and hard across the middle. Each man, stepping quickly to the plate as his turn came, "dumped" the first pitch slowly down one or the other of the base lines, then took three regular cuts at the ball. The boys were hitting, too; sharp line drives zipped over the infield, and red-hot skinners kept the shaggers dancing.

Even Bronc Burnett pasted a couple that would have been base hits during a game; a little high, perhaps, but well past the spots where infielders would most likely have been stationed.

That's swell! he thought. Sure feels good to bust 'em on the nose! No wonder Dad always liked to hit! Do you suppose he saw that last one? I'll bet he did, even though he's been pretending not to notice me. He saw it, all right! He's waving at me. That's what it takes to make Dad sit up and take notice: base hits!

Cap'n Al permitted Bronc to bat only once during the practice session, the rest of the time holding him on the bench to rest. Then, as Sonora relinquished the field for their visitors to hit, he slid onto the seat beside Bronc and laid a strong hand on his knee.

"You can start warming up now," the coach said quietly. "Take it easy; lots of stretching, lots of winding up. Get yourself thoroughly limber. You'll have about twenty minutes of slow work. Then when Lakewood has finished batting practice, and when you see us run out onto the field for our infield workout, why, that's when I want you to start the real throwing. Pour 'em in, then—just as if you were pitching a real game. Make every pitch count. Aim every one at a definite target; high and inside, low and outside, straight through the guts, and so on. Keep it up, steady, all the time we're taking our infield workout. By the time the rest of us have finished, I want to see sweat all over you. You can sit down, then, for a little while, as they take theirs.

"Go ahead now, and remember: start easy!"

Bronc almost leaped to his feet in eagerness. He whirled on the bulky, round-cheeked youth who had settled down on the other side of the coach. "Come on, Fat! Bring your mitt, fellow!"

But Cap'n Al shook his head, smiling.

"Do your preliminary warming up with George Fitzpatrick," he ordered. "Fat will catch you a few, just before game time, but I can't spare him now. We're going to sit here together and watch those Lakewood batters take their hitting practice, so he'll know what pitches to call during the game."

"Then Fat is going to catch me?"

The coach nodded.

Bronc would have stayed to congratulate Fat, who was beaming all over, but a curt motion from the very businesslike Cap'n Al sent him hurrying to his warmup.

Approximately thirty minutes later, Fat Crompton

came out to Bronc. Fat was sweating like a plow horse, and almost staggering from loss of breath, but on his face was a grin that wouldn't come off.

"I'll take over now, George," he announced. "Boy, we sure had a workout! How's Bronc looking?"

"Wonderful! His curve is breaking sharp, and he's got a fast ball that would make a rifle jealous."

Cap'n Al presently motioned Bronc and Fat to the bench for a brief rest.

Lakewood had followed Sonora with their infield practice, and now they had finished, too. A ground keeper hurried out to put the finishing touches on a few rough spots that had developed along the skinned base lines.

It was a perfect day for a game. Only a few high-flying clouds, and they were down-canyon to the east, with the sky above and to the west as clear and blue as a crystal. A brief shower on the day before had wetted the diamond just right; neither too fast, nor too dusty.

The stands had long been full. And stretched for perhaps a city block down both side lines were cars and trucks as close together as their drivers had been able to park them. Every car bumper and fender carried its capacity of baseball-eager fans; and back behind, looking over the tops of the cars, some forty or fifty cowboys eagerly watched from astride their ponies.

Promptly at three-thirty, the lanky figure of Sheriff Pole Drinkwater strode out to home plate. The Sheriff had discarded his customary big Stetson for a blue baseball cap. He had turned its bill backward over his neck, and a huge chest protector already covered his lawman's badge. He carried his mask in one hand and a brand-new baseball in the other.

He glanced briefly down at the ball, on which his notes had obviously been penciled, then turned and tilted his head toward the crowded stands behind home plate.

"Batteries for today's game: For Lakewood, Kimbrell and Stowe. For Sonora, Burnett and Crompton. *Play ball!*"

As though suddenly charged with electricity, the entire Sonora team, with the lone exception of Bronc Burnett, shot from their seats and dashed, chattering and yelling, onto the field. Somebody produced a ball. In a jiffy it was being whipped snappily back and forth.

Bronc Burnett and Cap'n Al Carter walked out to the mound together. The coach had his arm around Bronc, talking quietly, earnestly, as they walked:

"You've got the stuff to win this one, Burnett. I've got a lot of hope tied up in you. So has the team. Just forget the crowd, and pitch ball: forget everybody except your catcher and the batter. Later on, as we have more practice sessions, I'll begin to explain about a pitcher's other duties. But today I don't think it's going to be necessary. You're better than these Lakewood hitters, if you just keep your head and pitch ball."

They had reached the mound by this time. Cap'n Al hesitated a moment longer.

"Don't let the crowd get your goat today, Burnett. None of that rabbit ears stuff! Don't pay any attention to them at all."

"I won't!" Bronc promised. Despite some inner nervousness, the husky youngster managed to grin.

"That's the spirit! Now, just remember: You're out here for just one job only; to win a ball game for Sonora. Because if you don't—well—if I catch you paying any attention whatever to the crowd, so help me, I'll jerk you out of the game so fast your head will swim! But I don't think it will be necessary, boy. You learned your lesson last week. You've practiced hard, and you've got the stuff. Now, start shoving it through! And good luck!"

"Thanks, Coach! I won't let you down!"

Bronc turned to the plate. Fat Crompton was waiting for him, in chest protector and shin guards, his mask lying on the ground near by. Fat tossed him a new ball, then crouched. Bronc wound up, shot him a fast one. Fat grinned delightedly, pegged it back. Bronc threw another one.

There! That felt better. He could work this cussed nervousness off. Three more practice throws allowed. Okay, how about this one?

He wound up, reared back, and really turned the steam loose. The ball nearly tore Crompton's hand off, but the fat boy trapped it and winged it back, ready for another. Again Bronc shot his fast one. As he advanced a couple of steps to take Crompton's return throw, he flashed a quick look over toward the Lakewood bench. The players had their eyes on him, all right. Bulging eyes, Bronc noted.

Scared already! It gave him more confidence. By the time he had fired his final pitch across the plate, Bronc's nervousness was pretty well gone. He was ready. Ready, even, for Fibate Jones, or any other loudmouthed ya-hoot! They couldn't bother him today. He'd show 'em, if they tried it. And he'd show Dad, too. Dad and Cap'n Al, both. All right, let's get this thing started!

The team behind him had already begun to bark:

"Everybody alive now! Let's get number one! Who wants him? I'll take him. Make him hit to me, Bronc! Make him hit to me. . . ."

The umpire dusted off home plate, while Fat Crompton put on his mask. A sprightly, thin-shouldered little batsman stepped into the box, pounded home plate with his bat, rubbed one sleeve across his forehead, then crouched, close to the plate and bent low. He flashed a half-friendly grin at Bronc out on the mound, but Bronc did not return it.

He'd learned his lesson. He'd had his instructions. He

wasn't "fraternizing" with anybody today. Nobody but his catcher, Fat Crompton. He had a job to do, and he was going to do it! Cold-blooded, mechanical, all business.

"Everybody hustle in there, gang! Everybody alive! Make him hit to me, Bronc! Make him hit to me. . . ."

Now, let's see about this batter; lead-off man. Always fast, usually small, and always smart, Cap'n Al had said. Got to watch 'em—they're apt to draw a base on balls. Try to upset a pitcher first thing, and they'd rather get a base on balls than a hit.

What was Fat signaling?

Fast one, straight over.

Good stuff, Fat! That's right. Fat knows how to call 'em—Fat remembers. No good lead-off man ever takes a cut at the first pitch. The first pitch belongs to the pitcher. Well, if it's mine, here's where I get it. We'll put Mr. Lead-off Man in a hole with a called strike! Won't shove too much steam behind it. Don't need to. And, besides, it's better to ease up a little in order to cinch my control. Got to have this first strike. Can't put myself in the hole—that's for the batter!

"Let's go in there, Bronc! All behind you, big boy! All behind you! Make him hit to me. . . ."

The crowd, too, let out a roar as Bronc started his windup. The game was on.

And *suddenly!*

Before the crowd could draw a breath, the little lead-off man for Lakewood had taken a vicious swing at the ball, connected, and was on his way. Like shot from a cannon, the ball zoomed over Buck Losey's head on third and kicked up lime on the foul stripe far out in left field. Peedink Harrell gave chase, and Trail Drover—hustling, fighting little shortstop-captain for Sonora—raced out to help relay the throw back.

Trail's hustling action saved it from being a home run,

55

as he rifled the ball to Crompton in time to turn the Lakewood runner back to third.

Gradually a horrified roar faded from the stunned folks up in the stands.

Out on the mound, Bronc Burnett stamped around like a wounded grizzly. What kind of baseball was that, anyhow? Somebody ought to show that little "country jake" how a lead-off man should act! Who ever heard of such a thing—landing on the first pitched ball of a game? And if—

What was that? "Illegal!" did somebody say?

Bronc, with the ball now returned to his glove, stood squarely on the pitching slab waiting for the next hitter. But as the word "illegal" came distinctly to his ears once more, he allowed his angry glance to shift to the side line between home and first.

There—in front of the Lakewood bench! A tall man in overalls was yelling something to him. He came closer to the base line, motioning emphatically at Bronc. But Bronc, for all his curiosity, turned his eyes again toward home plate. That's what counted: the batter. Never mind the crowd. He'd promised Cap'n Al—

"Come on out there, Pitcher!" he heard the man in overalls yell. "You can't pull that stuff! It's illegal!"

What in thunder did the fellow mean, anyhow? Bronc continued to study the batter, who had now stepped to the plate, but his ears were all for the accusing man in overalls.

"You're doctoring the ball! You're using emery!" the fellow charged loudly. "That isn't fair!"

So that was it!

Bronc grinned in relief. "No, I'm not using anything!" he replied, glancing toward the other. "See?" He held up the ball.

"Yeah, but it's all *rough!* You doctored it! Throw it here. I'll prove it! We want a square deal, Mr. Pitcher!"

Square deal? Why, the insinuating yip-yap! Bronc

56

felt a rush of hot blood to his face. He'd never cheated in his life, and he wasn't cheating now.

"I never did anything to the ball!" he snapped.

"Yes, you did! I can prove it! Throw it here!"

Bewildered, angry, Bronc hesitated. The whole thing had happened fast. He glanced down at the ball instinctively to reassure himself. It was slick as glass, not a scratch on it. The noisy stranger was mistaken. He might—

"Throw it here! I'll prove it!" Bronc heard him challenge again.

Bronc wavered. His worried glance shifted down to his glove, then once more to the accusing stranger between first and home. Convinced the man was wrong, he was half in mind to toss him the ball. But another yell, this time from the Sonora side of the field, drew his attention. He turned.

There was Cap'n Al, motioning angrily: "Don't throw the ball to that yahoot! It's a trick! He'll jump out of the way, and the runner on third will score. You play the batter!"

Bronc grinned in genuine relief.

"Sure, Coach! Thanks!"

Gosh! He'd nearly messed that one! Good thing Cap'n Al had been around!

Once more Bronc faced the batter. He took Crompton's signal, made the stretch, started his throw. But in the last fleet instant before Bronc turned it loose, again the shrill scream of the man in overalls:

"The *bicycle!* Oh, look out! The *bicycle!*"

Bronc's pitch, a high fast one, was deflected the merest trifle—but enough that it zipped far above Crompton's mitt into the screen sixty feet behind the plate. Crompton hurled his mask aside and gave chase, while Bronc rushed to cover home, but the runner from third scored easily.

Bronc whirled on the umpire, shoving his chin almost

57

in lanky Pole Drinkwater's face. "You can't allow that!" he protested. "That was interference by—"

Slowly Drinkwater took off his mask. He removed Bronc's grip from his sleeves, and resolutely shook his head.

"I'm plumb sorry, lad," he said, "but it will have to go as a plain wild pitch. Nobody else was anywhere near you—you were in position. So the run counts. Now, go on back, and play ball!"

Bronc turned around, stunned. But then he saw something else that set his heart to pounding even faster.

Lefty Lear was out on the mound. Lefty—and beside him, Cap'n Al Carter. The coach had one arm up over his new pitcher's shoulder. Bronc knew what it meant. Slowly he turned to the bench.

Chapter 5

CAP'N AL OBJECTS

BASEBALL was serious business in Sonora.

They told Bronc afterward that the crowd raised quite a rumpus as he stumbled dejectedly to the bench, but at the time he was too stunned to notice anything. Folks were about evenly divided: some thought he had deserved a longer stay on the mound, while others, obviously still smarting from the way he and Fat Crompton had tossed away the preceding game, were furious enough to have boiled him in oil.

He found the bench and dazedly sat down. All around him bedlam continued, but it was unintelligible.

Bronc shuddered, remembering something else: "That's *my* kid out there pitching!" he had mimicked to his father. And: "I won't let you be ashamed of me again. . . ."

Somewhere up in those howling stands his father would be sitting. Sitting, like Bronc, with his chin in his hands, and neither seeing nor caring what else happened out there on the diamond. Again Bronc's own words, not four hours old, returned to mock him:

"That's *my* kid out there pitching!"

Bronc straightened slowly, got wearily to his feet. He would go to the gym and change clothes. Get rid of this fateful uniform—get away from this mob. Let 'em holler at somebody else a while. Yeah—let 'em holler at Lefty.

Lefty wouldn't like it, either. He'd probably blow up, too. Then so would Red Bailey, their only other pitcher. Then who would Cap'n Al send to the mound? He'll be sorry then, I betcha. He'll wish he hadn't been so fast at yanking me.

"Hey, down there! Hey, Rabbit Ears! Hey, why don't you go hide? Hey, you can't play ball—why don't you . . ."

Gradually it dawned on Bronc that the words were being leveled at him. He turned toward the grandstand, noting half a dozen jeering faces on the lower row. Wasp Dillon was there among them. Wasp and some more of his breed.

"Hey, Rabbit Ears, why don't you try out for the girls' embroidery team?"

Bronc Burnett never knew how he did it, but from somewhere he managed to produce a grin. He even waved at the group. "There'll be other games!" he yelled, with far more confidence than he could possibly feel.

"Yeah, but you won't be in 'em!"

Slowly, Bronc turned his back on the group. His head came up. Once more he started for the Sonora bench. This time his stride was positive and rapid. He wouldn't leave. Let them hoot till their lungs were sore. He'd stay right here and take it. Besides, maybe the team would need him. He couldn't re-enter the line-up, of course, but maybe there'd be something he could do.

Somebody flopped down beside him. "Tough luck, pardner!" A set of fingers gripped his leg.

Bronc glanced around. His eyes widened. "You—Fat? What's he taking you out for?"

"For a better man, I reckon."

"But it wasn't your fault! Gosh, Fat—I hate this! It's bad enough for me to fizzle, but to splash mud on you, too—gee, that's awful! You were counting a lot on this game, yourself, weren't you? And because of me—"

60

"Skip it! We'll get another chance Friday. That's only day after tomorrow. And we'll make these noisy coyotes eat their words yet!"

"We will, if we get the chance. But I'd bet that Cap'n Al never gives us another try. Besides, in another week Pitch Carson will be ready to play again."

"You'll be better than Pitch someday," Fat Crompton predicted. "Of course, we may have to stuff your ears with cotton ahead of each game."

"Let's see how Lefty gets along!"

They watched Lefty Lear complete his warmup throws to Drake Yoder, the regular catcher, who had been recalled from his temporary station in right field. Johnny Hall went to right. And down the third-base line, far enough so it wouldn't disturb the pitcher, Red Bailey began warming up with George Fitzpatrick.

"Play ball!"

Cap'n Al Carter came back to the bench. It was out of his hands now. Up to the nine lads out there on the diamond. Bronc slid over to make room, but the coach ignored him and sat nearer the end. The team went into its jargon:

"What do you say in there, gang? Everybody alive now! Make him hit to me, Lefty! Make him hit to me. . . ."

Lefty Lear was a gangling, loose-jointed six-footer, with coal-black hair and eyes. He was nervous by nature, and today on the mound he seemed even more so than usual. His hands were constantly in motion, rubbing the ball, rubbing his pants, rubbing his forehead . . . all the time, fidgeting and scratching the dirt with his spikes.

Now he toed the slab, took a quick look at the signal Drake Yoder was giving him, and windmilled his long arms in an awkward windup.

It was a wild pitch, so high that his catcher couldn't have batted it down with a shovel.

A groan went up from the crowd. Drake Yoder hobbled out to speak with Lefty for a moment, slapped him on the back, pressed a ball into his hand, then trotted back to his position behind the plate.

Lefty's second pitch was better, though it went for "Ball two!" Drake had caught it, high and outside.

Then Lefty Lear seemed to find the range. His next throw got a corner for a called strike. The batter helped by nibbling at a low curve on the following try. But there Lefty got himself into trouble again. "Ball three!" on one that hit the dirt in front of the plate; and "Ball four!" on a feeble-looking pitch that Drake Yoder took with his bare hand far to the right of its target.

The crowd seethed uneasily as a big right-hander strode confidently to the plate.

But an instant later they broke into a roar of approval. Lefty Lear, with the deceptive motion natural to left-handed pitchers, had suddenly trapped the runner off first.

There! One away now—the bases clean! That's better! Guess Cap'n Al knew what he was doing, after all. The kid's a pitcher, all right. Can't pick runners off first on luck—got to know how. Might have been nervous at the start, but he's got his wits about him now. This big brute looks tough, but Lefty'll get him out. Come on, Lefty!

"Too bad we didn't have Lefty in there at the beginning!" Bronc heard Fibate Jones tell somebody behind him.

But Bronc paid no attention. He was learning!

The big Lakewood batter swung at Lefty's first pitch, connected, and sent a mighty fly deep into center field. Bill Burnham had been off with the crack of the bat, however, and pulled it down handily.

Two away! Nice going, boys! They'll back you up, Lefty! Stay in there and pitch, boy!

However, Lefty promptly lapsed into another wild streak. He walked the next two batters on eight pitched balls. And as "Ball one!" sounded on the next, threatening to continue the string, again Drake Yoder came out briefly to steady him.

The ensuing pitch, a half-speed attempt, straight across the middle, found the big batsman ready. He swung from the heels, smashing a line drive at "Slow Molasses" Smith on first. Smith managed to knock the ball down, but was too late to beat the runner to base.

"The pitcher oughta covered first on that play!" Wasp Dillon's voice shrieked from the stands. "Hey, Lefty! Get alive out there, and—"

Bronc Burnett leaped to his feet. "Cut out that talk!" he bellowed, whirling to face Wasp and his group. "Leave Lefty alone! He's already got his hands full try-to beat Lakewood, without having to worry with the home folks, too!"

"Hey! If Lefty—"

"If you wolves want to chew on somebody, why don't you take a few more bites out of me!"

They did—with apparent relish!

And despite his resolve not to let it bother him, their fusillade of verbal barbs stung Bronc to the quick. But he did not attempt to hand any of it back. He merely returned to the bench and took his seat, apparently oblivious to everything except the play on the diamond. However, he did notice that their venom was all directed at him now. They were leaving Lefty alone.

For the first time since pulling Bronc from the game, Cap'n Al Carter glanced his way. It seemed, momentarily, that his icy manner toward the boy might change, but again he turned his head, and again his face was hard and unrelenting.

Bases full! Out on the mound, Lefty Lear was more nervous than ever. The team tried to help:

"Never mind that, Lefty! Glad the sacks are loaded —makes it all the easier to get the big one! Just tag any base, gang! Never mind home plate—the run won't count, anyhow—just tag any base. . . ."

But the Lakewood team had shot its bolt. The timid-looking little fellow who came to bat now, hitting in sixth place, could have drawn an easy base on balls by waiting; but instead he took two ridiculous swings at low, wide curves, and then popped an easy fly to Chic Stahl on second.

"You can see why they're in last place," Fat Crompton whispered hoarsely to Bronc. "They've only got five hitters. Once you get past those five, you get a breathing spell for an inning or so. Cap'n Al noticed that during their practice. I wouldn't be surprised if Lefty beats them—bad as he is."

"He isn't so bad. He'll get going. Let's help to keep his chin up!"

The Sonora team came racing to the bench.

"Come on, gang! They've only got one run on us—shouldn't have got that! Now let's get it back! Let's get a dozen! Let's get a lead for Lefty! Lefty can't win it alone! Let's get him a lead. . . ."

Peedink Harrell was first up. The little fellow took his peculiar, hunched-over stance and faced the Lakewood pitcher. Strike one—called. Ball one. Ball two. Ball three. Then one straight over the middle. Peedink watched it without moving. Now for the three-two pitch.

"Ball four!"

The crowd made a lot of noise over that—part of it cheering, but a plentiful sprinkling of guffaws, too. The little fellow could sure draw those bases on balls. Hard to pitch to, all right. Sure glad he's on our side, especially if our pitcher is going to be wilder than a drunk sheepherder.

Suddenly another buzz broke from the lower stands. Wasp Dillon and his group had recognized Sonora's new bat boy.

"Hey, out there!" went the cry. "Hey, Rabbit Ears! So you're gonna be a bat boy, are you? Hey, Rabbit Ears —what'll you try next, if you can't carry bats?"

Bronc Burnett heard them, all right. Never had his rabbit ears worked better, and he flushed to the roots of his hair, but otherwise he gave not the slightest sign that he heard. Calmly he retrieved the bat that Peedink Harrell had dropped on his way to first, paused to give Chic Stahl an encouraging slap on the back, and ran back to the Sonora bench.

"Hey, Rabbit Ears! We thought you'd go off some place and die! Why don't you—"

Fat Crompton laid his hand on Bronc's knee. "Never mind them, pardner! Don't let them get your goat!"

"They're not bothering me. Besides, I wonder if it isn't good practice?" Bronc chuckled. "Wouldn't it get *their* goats if they knew it was really helping me?"

"You might have something there! If a fellow's hide gets tough enough to withstand Fibate and Wasp Dillon, he won't have trouble anywhere else! Look! Isn't that a beauty?"

Chic Stahl, batting in second place today, had just dumped a neat bunt down the third-base line. The Lakewood pitcher dashed over and managed to get his throw to first ahead of Chic, but the play had sacrificed little Peedink Harrell easily to second.

Bronc hurried to the plate, gathered up the bat, and returned to the bench.

The wolves along the bottom row let him alone this time, being more engrossed in the fact that Sonora now had a nimble runner in scoring position, with only one down.

"Come on, Smitty! Give the old apple a ride, you big lazy ham!"

Smith did. It went for three bases. Driven solidly between right and center, it would have been a home run for any other man on the team, but the big first baseman barely managed to make third, where he stood puffing and panting from the run. Peedink had scored easily.

Tied up now, one and one. And Bill Burnham was up, with a man waiting on third.

"I'll bet Bill brings him in!" Fat Crompton predicted eagerly. "Bill's a good man in a pinch—Bill never lets his team down."

"Not like me, eh?"

"Aw, I didn't mean that, Bronc! You know I didn't! Doggone it, those rabbit ears of yours never sleep, do they? If you ever— There! Look at that! What did I tell you?" Fat pounded Bronc on the back. "Holy cow! Did Bill really knock the seams off that one! And here comes Smith—looks like a locomotive, the way he's puffing, but it counts us a run, just the same. Good boy, Molasses!"

Bronc was already off the bench. He side-stepped long enough to give Smith a pat, then hurriedly recovered the bat that Bill Burnham had tossed aside. Starting back to the bench, however, Bronc was mildly surprised to see that Smith had stopped and was waiting for him.

"Thanks, Bronc!"

Smith went on to the bench.

But Bronc Burnett stood riveted in his tracks. Did you hear that, fellow? "Thanks, Bronc!" the big first baseman had said, presumably in response to Bronc's congratulatory pat on making the run. Then Smitty wasn't sore at him! He had one friend left, at least, besides Fat Crompton. How that helped! And how thankful, now, that he hadn't left the field to change clothes—wouldn't that have been awful? Yellow, they'd have figured him— didn't have the nerve to stay and take it. Well, he could take it, all right. He'd show 'em! He could take all that "Fibate, Wasp & Company" could throw in his direction. Take it, and call for more! And the next time Cap'n Al Carter gave him a chance to pitch—*Cap'n Al!*

The name jerked Bronc back to earth.

Cap'n Al hadn't even spoken to him since the game started. Furthermore, he had seemed to be purposely

66

avoiding him; not only sat at the opposite end of the bench, but he didn't even watch as Bronc returned each time to lay a bat in front of him. The coach was sore, all right.

For the remainder of that inning, Bronc Burnett was the busiest man on the team. Batter after batter hit safely, or walked, or reached first on an error. And by the time the wild orgy was over, eleven runs had crossed the plate, and the third pitcher was vainly toiling for Lakewood.

Sonora raced onto the field.

"Eleven to one in our favor now, gang! We've got you a nice lead now, Lefty! Let's hold 'em in there, boy! Everybody alive! Make 'em hit to me! Let me have number one. . . . "

Lakewood went out in order. The first man popped a foul, which Drake Yoder caught just behind home plate, the second grounded out, unassisted, to Smith on first, and the third swung wildly at Lefty Lear's sweeping curves.

"What did I tell you?" Fat Crompton jabbered to Bronc on the bench. "Cap'n Al has them figured, all right. Once you get past their top five, it's easy sailing. Those bottom four couldn't hit a bull in the head with a shovel!"

Bronc nodded grimly. "It makes me want to kick my own rear end! I should have pitched this game. Should have been out there the full nine innings. And, boy, with that much practice under my belt, I would have been ready for—"

"You know," Fat cut in seriously, "I've just been wondering, ever since that loudmouthed, overalled gent pulled his shenanigans on you: maybe it's a good thing."

"In the name of common sense, why?"

"Because the team isn't going to need you today. On Friday, against Hope, they will! Hope's in sixth place, and fairly good with the stick. You know, the more I think about it, the more I believe Cap'n Al is secretly glad he had to pull you—and consequently, save you for Friday's game. Not only will you be fresh and strong, but you've learned another darn good lesson."

"Are you telling me?" muttered Bronc.

At the end of six innings of play, a tall, scholarly-looking man rose from the Lakewood bench and came over to Cap'n Al Carter. He wore a tired smile, and was slowly shaking his head.

"It's twenty-three to three," he said, "so, according to conference rules, we must concede you the game. Being new, perhaps no one has told you: when one team has a lead of more than fifteen runs at any time after the sixth inning, the game shall be declared 'terminated and complete.'"

"No, sir. I wasn't familiar with that."

"Then I'll have the umpire call it off. And may I congratulate you, Mr. Carter. You have a hustling team. They will cause trouble for any of the leaders, if you can find added strength on the mound." The Lakewood coach held out his hand.

"Thank you, sir!" Cap'n Al gripped his hand briefly, then with an abruptness that was almost rude, he turned. "If you'll excuse me, please, there's a man around here—somewhere—that I've got some urgent business with."

"Why, of course."

Bronc Burnett, who had been waiting for some word with the coach, tensed eagerly as Cap'n Al started straight for him. But Cap'n Al, his eyes on the crowd far beyond, had no such notion. He had edged past Bronc, when Bronc spoke to him:

"If it's okay with you, sir, I'd like to come out for practice tomorrow as usual? I still think—"

Cap'n Al did not even glance toward him. He continued on, hurrying even faster, and presently overtook a tall man in overalls, who was lingering on the edge of the crowd. Bronc saw him catch the tall man by a shirt sleeve. It was the same noisy meddler who had caused him to wild pitch in the first inning!

The stranger was at least two inches taller than Cap'n Al, and perhaps ten years younger, but they looked to be about the same in weight. And from the flushed faces of both, and their all-round air of belligerency, much like two dogs eying one another—stiff-legged and on tip-toes—it seemed as if their physical equality might really be tested, and soon!

"I waited until the game was over," Bronc heard Cap'n Al tell the stranger, "because I didn't want any ruckus to interfere with a Sonora victory. Now I have a few things to lay on the line to you."

The tall stranger shoved Cap'n Al's fingers from his arm. "I don't carry any sign that says 'Keep Off'!" he sneered. "If you've got any business with me, there's no-body sittin' on your shirttail!"

Cap'n Al's cold eyes narrowed, but when he spoke his voice was still steady.

"You pulled some dirty tactics on one of my boys, just as the game started. I didn't like it. I still don't. They're just kids, and I'm trying to teach them sports-manship as well as baseball."

"It ain't a matter of sportsmanship at all!" the other argued. "I don't know where you ever played ball, but I can tell you this: In baseball, you play to win. Any-thing goes! None of this sissy, you-first-please stuff—you grab every break you can."

"In pay ball, yes. On your own little town teams around here, too, probably. But not in high school! My boys play hard, but they play clean. And their oppo-nents are going to do the same thing. That's why I say, your tactics were a poor example. And I don't like it!"

"In that case, maybe you'd like to do something about it?" the tall man suggested.

He shifted his weight slightly, shoving his left shoul-

69

der out toward Cap'n Al, and lowering to a partial crouch.

"Frankly, I would! But that wouldn't help."

"Maybe this will!"

The tall man's left hand streaked forward. Its open palm caught Cap'n Al a noisy smack on the cheek. He danced nimbly backward, both fists doubled now, openly inviting Cap'n Al to have a try.

He got results in a hurry!

Drawn by the shouts of the crowd, Sheriff Drinkwater was on the spot in less than a minute, and hauled the two apart. But that had been, perhaps, the longest minute of the tall stranger's life to date! Bystanders helped him to limp away, and somebody loaned him a handkerchief to press against his badly smashed lips.

"Who was that big gorilla?" he mumbled dazedly.

Cap'n Al replaced his baseball cap, dusted one sleeve, then turned to the crowd.

"It's all right for *me* to raise Ned with my boys," he said soberly, "and I expect to do plenty of it. They'll either hustle, or I'll bust 'em over the rump with a wet rope! But don't let me ever catch an outsider meddling with one of them!" He singled out five or six of the team who were clustered together. "We'll practice at two-thirty tomorrow, sharp!"

"Does that include me, too, sir?" Bronc inquired.

The coach eyed him sternly. "I said, at two-thirty tomorrow, sharp! Isn't that clear, or do I have to draw you a picture?"

Bronc swallowed a lump in his throat, as tears of gratitude threatened to fog his eyes.

Chapter 6

BURNETT, RIGHT FIELD

THURSDAY'S practice, as usual, started in a spirited way. Lots of chatter, half a dozen balls in the air at once, everybody full of pep. And why shouldn't they be? Tied for second, weren't they? Only a notch behind Spur!

Spur had beaten Greenfield on the day before, and now had the only clean slate in the conference. Slug Langenegger, so word came back to them, had knocked a grand-slam homer in the ninth with two away, converting an almost certain four-to-one defeat into a spectacular five-to-four victory.

The only rub: they wouldn't get another crack at Spur. Somebody else would have to pin Spur's ears back, if Sonora were to advance.

Meanwhile, there was Hope to pass tomorrow. Hope had beaten Suerte yesterday while Sonora was winning over Lakewood, and now stood at two won and two lost. They were reported to have a fine team defensively, but so far hadn't scored more than four runs in any of their games.

"All right, Burnett—you and Crompton," Cap'n Al ordered after the preliminary warmup. "We're going to have hitting practice today until your knees drag. That's the best way to handle these so-called defensive teams:

concentrate on their pitchers, and smash 'em off the field. Let's go!"

Bronc trotted to the mound, and Fat behind the plate. They started easy, but it wasn't five minutes until Bronc was laying the ball across with plenty of speed.

Meanwhile, Cap'n Al had gone off down the side lines with Red Bailey and Drake Yoder. He spent a lot of time with Red, coaching him tirelessly on a pitcher's stance, delivery, and follow-through. Then he returned to watch the hitting.

"You can come out of there now," he said to Bronc finally. "I'll toss a few over myself. Lefty Lear isn't in shape, and I'm saving Red."

Neither Bronc nor Fat had a dry stitch of clothing above the waist, as they trudged wearily to the side lines. Fat promptly rolled over on his back, arms lying limply beside him, his barrel-like chest heaving exhaustedly, but Bronc picked out a bat and crouched on one knee beside it. Presently, during a lull when Cap'n Al was waiting for a ball to be returned, he got up and walked closer.

"How about giving me a cut?" he asked.

"Okay. You follow Drake."

When Bronc's turn came, he faced the pitcher eagerly. It would be in there, he knew, because the former leaguer still had wonderful control, and each pitch was squarely across the middle with just enough steam to give it a ride.

Cap'n Al fired the ball across. Bronc met it straight on the nose. It looped lazily toward center field, where one of the shaggers caught it. Again Cap'n Al pitched, and again Bronc hit—this time, a medium-sized bounder to short.

Bronc stepped back from the plate momentarily, a frown of disgust on his face. "Everything I hit carries handles on it—easy outs. Why in thunder can't I put some power behind them? At anything else I'm strong as a mule, but even little Peedink can hit a ball farther."

"It's your timing," the coach told him. "You're not hitting, you're pushing the ball. Besides, I think maybe you're crowding too close to the plate. Stand back a little farther, then you'll be leaning into the pitch. Now, let's try it again, and this time, wait until the very last before you swing. Then swing fast. Act like you're mad at it!"

The pitch. The swing. A high pop-up foul nearly straight above home plate.

"You didn't watch the ball! Keep your eye on it, right up until the time it actually connects with the bat!"

Bronc did a little better on the next two; one a blooper behind first, which might have gone for a single, the other a fairly solid drive straight back at the pitcher. He then relinquished the bat to Bill Burnham.

Before pitching any more, however, Cap'n Al came down to the plate. He tossed his glove aside, picking up a bat instead.

"There's no ironclad rule about hitting," he said, as a dozen eager youngsters promptly clustered about him. "From somewhere, sometime, a case can be dug up to disprove any rule ever made. Take Al Simmons, for instance: Al used to step into the bucket the worst way. We tell young players not to do it, that it's positively wrong, and that they'll only get horse collars instead of a batting average. And yet, this one player, back in the early thirties, was probably the greatest batter of his time. But look how awkward it would be for anybody else—"

Cap'n Al took the stance, about three-quarters facing an imaginary pitcher. He swung slowly, stepping back with his left foot.

"See? It wouldn't work for me at all, and I don't want to catch any of you trying it, either! But, while we're on the subject of unusual ways to bat, here's the way Babe Ruth used to stand."

He stepped to the left-hand side of the plate, this time

almost turning his back to the mound and peering over his right shoulder at a supposed pitcher. Again he swung, slowly to illustrate, cocking his right foot, and driving into an imaginary ball with all his weight on the left.

"I wouldn't advise that one either," he grinned, "even though it produced 729 big-league home runs. And here's another extreme: Hack Wilson, who used to be with the old Chicago Cubs back in the late twenties; Hack always stood with his feet spread wide apart and parallel to the plate, but so far away from it you wouldn't think his bat could ever reach one on the outside. As I remember, he never stepped into a ball, or even moved his feet when he swung, just kept them as still as if they were anchored in concrete. Hack did all of his hitting with his arms and shoulders, and he was muscled like a buffalo."

"But isn't he noted more for his strike-outs than for his batting?" Bronc Burnett asked. "It seems as though I've read where he whiffed more times than anybody else in his league."

"He did, I'll grant. But he also led the entire league in runs-batted-in. And, let me tell you, lads, that's where the real payoff in baseball comes—in a man's ability to drive his teammates across the plate with scores. The knack, or the courage, call it what you will, of being able to 'hit in the clutch,' as we say, counts more than a mere Fancy-Dan batting average.

"But I started to show you what is generally regarded as the best all-round hitting form.

"In the first place," Cap'n Al continued, "the bat should be held quite firmly. Not too tight, of course, or it will tense your wrist and arm muscles and cramp your swing. It must be swung parallel to the ground, neither chopping down, like a man trying to kill a snake, nor swinging upward, like a golfer does. Keep it straight. And before the pitch gets to you, while you're waiting, it's best to have most of your weight on your back foot. As the ball gets close, and you want to swing, step quickly forward with your front foot just an instant before you actually swing. Then, as you connect, put all the power you have into your wrists and arms. You've already thrown your body weight into the ball when you leaned forward.

"And be sure to follow through—don't just connect. Follow through, all the way. Are there any questions?"

After a short silence, Fat Crompton held up his hand.

"Do you follow the same tactics for hitting a curve?"

"In general, yes. You hold back, always, as long as you dare. Then you lash out quick when the ball gets in range, reaching out more with your arms in the case of a curve. It will depend, also, on how long or how short a grip you happen to have on the bat. Ruth always took the longest possible grip. Ty Cobb, the old Detroit star, used to catch his much shorter—'choking' the bat, we call it—most often used by men who are place hitters rather than sluggers. But we'll go into that later. There's plenty yet to come!" Cap'n Al grinned wryly. "A fellow never learns everything about baseball. And by the time he's learned most of the fundamentals, he's probably so old that some green rookie with a lot of fire and speed comes along and shoves him off!

"Oh, yes!" he recalled suddenly. "Something else I nearly forgot, which is mighty important: don't ever try to outguess a pitcher. The odds are too much against it. Besides, you're apt to get hit by a ball if you guess wrong. So just stand there and wait for the pitch, and be sure you're ready to swing, or to duck, or to let it go by.

"I'll throw for another ten minutes' hitting practice," he concluded, "and then I want you, Red, to take the box. We need to run through a few plays where the pitcher has to cover first base. We lost an 'out' yesterday on that. And by the way, we'll start work on signals next week. I'm afraid to give them to you now—we've crammed too much already into our sessions. We'll just concentrate on outhitting Hope tomorrow. If they get a run, we'll get two; if they get two, we'll go after three."

"And if they get fifty," put in Fibate Jones, with a significant look toward Bronc Burnett, "we'll need fifty-one!"

Bronc grinned instantly. Then chuckled out loud. What the heck—can't bother me! That's kid stuff, that boloney about rabbit ears. Let these wolves try all they want to. They'll just be wasting breath. I'm going out to that mound tomorrow and I'm going to pitch ball—really shove that old apple through there like a comet. If they start chewing on me from the stands, I won't even hear it. But if I do hear it, it won't matter. My job is out there on the mound, not trying to win debates from "Fibate, Wasp & Company." I'll show 'em tomorrow. I'll pitch 'em a game they won't forget.

Gee, Im sorry Dad won't be here. He's seen me flop twice. He'd see something else tomorrow. Oh, well, he can read about it. Somebody will tell him, sure. And there'll be other games. I'm off on the right foot now. You just wait and see, Fibate, you loudmouthed little stinker! You little—

Gosh! There I go again! I wasn't going to let him get my goat. Well, he can't, when I get out there on the mound. I'll show him. I'll show 'em all!

"You know," Fat Crompton confided to Bronc, as they walked slowly to the dressing room nearly an hour later, "if I'm any judge of baseball, we're going to trim that Hope bunch hands down."

"They're in fourth place, only half a game behind us."

"I know. But the way our gang is knocking the cover off of the ball, we're bound to get some runs. And with your stuff on the mound, coupled with the fact that they're weak in batting anyhow, we might even shut them out."

"I'll certainly pitch my head off, if Cap'n Al will just give me another chance."

"He will!" Fat predicted confidently. "He knows you've got the stuff."

"But he doesn't know that I've completely whipped my rabbit ears jinx. You know—hearing too much from the crowd."

Fat grinned impishly. "Have you whipped it?"

"You wait and see!"

It was another fine day at game time, and a huge crowd was again on hand early. This would be the last home game for three weeks, so despite the fact they had seen their team in action only two days before, the baseball-hungry folks of Sonora were very much in evidence.

Bronc Burnett had been warming up ahead of time, and near by, Red Bailey was getting the kinks out of his arm. Presently Cap'n Al strolled over. He stood watching them closely for a few minutes. Then it happened:

"Red, I'm starting you today. Burnett, you will take right field."

Momentarily Bronc's chin sagged down onto his chest. But gradually a slow grin began to brighten his sandy, squarish features. "You mean, the other way around, don't you?"

"I mean just what I said: You will be in right, hitting seventh behind Trail Drover."

Again Bronc sobered. "Very well, sir!" He turned to leave, hesitated, then glanced back sharply toward the coach. "Do you mind if I ask, sir, is this some of my dad's doings?"

"What do you mean?"

Bronc reddened uneasily. "Aw, well—you see, Dad has always had his heart set on me being what he was—a slugging outfielder. Personally, I've gone one hundred per cent for this pitching job myself. So I just couldn't help wondering if he had told you—"

Cap'n Al Carter laughed. It was a low, deep laugh, the way a man laughs when something isn't funny.

"Listen, Burnett, I have the greatest respect for your

77

father. He is a fine man, and from what I hear he used to be a great athlete. But get yourself a load of this: Nobody—not even the President of the United States—is going to tell Alfred Krofts Carter how to run his ball club. So hustle yourself out there in right field before I kick the seat of your pants clear up through your neck!" But the coach accompanied his words with a grin, which now seemed to be friendly again.

Bronc trotted to his new position, as the rest of the team hurried to theirs. The game was on.

The first batter worked Red Bailey for a three-two count, then sent a looping grounder to short, which Drover grabbed easily and fired to Smith for a put-out. The next man singled sharply between first and second. Bronc came in at a dead run, scooped up the ball, and short-tossed to Chic Stahl on the keystone. Then he turned and hastily retreated to position.

"Come on in there, Red, boy! Make him hit to me!"

The batter might have heard! At any rate, he pumped Red Bailey's first pitch on a line into right field, about halfway between Bronc's position and the foul line. It looked like a certain three-bagger. But Bronc had ducked his head and started sprinting the instant he saw the ball start. And in that last split second, just before the drive reached him, he gave a mighty lunge and stretched his gloved hand as high and as far as it would reach.

There! He'd tipped it! The ball was still in the air!

He sprang again. Once more his fingers knocked the ball upward, but this time he grabbed it when it came down. He whirled. Sure enough, the man on first had figured it a safe hit and had broken for second. Now he had turned, and was racing back to first. Bronc fired the ball with a savagery that nearly lifted "Slow Molasses" Smith from the bag. Smith caught it, all right, and was in plenty of time to retire the runner, but the Hope man bumped him unexpectedly, and he dropped the ball.

Shoulda had three! But that's two down, anyhow!

78

Not your fault out there, Bronc! The stands fairly shook as the delighted crowd bellowed and stamped approval of his brilliant play. Now, let's get the last one out, boys!

Bronc was already back in position. He saw the next man approach the plate; a short, stocky fellow with thickset shoulders and powerful-looking arms. Clean-up man. Probably their longest hitter. Well, he certainly looked the part. Either hit it on the nose, or fan. Okay, suppose he should catch the ball on the meaty part of the bat; where would it be most likely to go? To center, under normal conditions. But with Red Bailey pitching— Red didn't have anything but a fast ball and good control —okay, suppose the batter then connected with Red's fast one; where would it go? He was right-handed, would swing a trifle slow—then to right field, of course! To *me!* All right, let it come. Believe I'll back up a little, though . . . say about twenty-five or thirty feet . . . the gent is hitting clean-up. Wouldn't be hitting there in fourth if he weren't a distance clouter. Here— This ought to get him. Now if he'll just poke it where he is supposed to!

Red Bailey took a look at first, then delivered the ball to the batter. It was wide of the plate, not far enough to get past Drake Yoder, but enough that the dancing, little runner on first thought he could make second. Ball and baseman arrived together. Dust fogged upward. Every eye in the park swung to the umpire. His hand came up, thumb extended.

"Runner's out! He missed the base!"

The Sonora team came scampering in to their bench. Peedink Harrell, first up, selected his bat and hurried over within a few feet of home plate. Chic Stahl was on deck. Smith in the hole.

Bronc Burnett sat down beside the coach.

"Nice catch out there, Burnett! Nice catch and throw!"

"Aw, it wasn't anything. Right in my glove. But, thank you, sir!"

He wondered how Fibate would feel toward him now? Fibate, and that other little squirt with the barbed-wire tongue, Wasp Dillon? Bronc wanted to look, would have given worlds for just one sideway look, but he couldn't now. That would be playing the crowd. He was through with that stuff. And what's more, when he finally took the mound again, he still wouldn't pay any heed whatever. Took the mound again—

Bronc sucked in his breath involuntarily. Would he ever get to pitch again? Or would Cap'n Al keep him in the outfield? In the field, it seemed likely. Especially, since "Pitch" Carson, the injured senior, would be ready to take over his old position by next week. Then there would be a scramble for the right-field position. "Nice catch and throw!" the coach had said to him. Well, that probably cinched it; no more pitching. He'd be a regular fielder from now on. He'd be shagging flies and concentrating on getting his base knocks from here on, instead of trying to outsmart enemy batsmen.

That would please his father, anyway. Dad didn't think much of pitchers; that is, in the endless conflict of Pitcher vs. Batter. So if his boy made the outfield and consequently became an enemy of all pitchers— Yes, Dad would be pleased to know that he was going to be a regular outfielder now.

A week ago the realization would have set Bronc's own pulse to jumping. But now—well—somehow a part of the thrill he had expected was lacking. And if—

A sudden groan from the crowd announced that the impossible had happened: Peedink Harrell had struck out!

Chic Stahl was hitting second.

"Come on, Chic! Get hold of one! Save me a turn, old fellow. . . ."

The Hope pitcher was a small boy, slender of body,

and slender of arms, but in the face he looked old, and he had the pitching poise of a veteran. He took his time now, eying the batter as he approached the plate, then turning for a check of his teammates' positions before starting to work on Chic Stahl.

Chic drove a grounder with a "base hit" label straight through the box and over second, but the visitors' short-stop raced toward it, speared it one-handed, and threw to first on a dead run. Out by a step! The infield peppered the ball around for a moment, chattering like a group of magpies, then tossed it to the slim pitcher.

"They're going to be tough, all right," Red Bailey muttered to Bronc, on the Sonora bench. "You might expect them to beat Smitty to first on a play like that, but Chic— Well, Chic's fast."

"Yeah, Chic's fast. But we'll whip 'em yet! How's your arm?"

"Good. But they're gonna be tough, I tell you."

Smith, the Sonora first baseman, slowly walked to the plate and took a lazy, seemingly careless stance. He was onto his business, however, and the nonchalant slouch deceived the Hope pitcher into grooving the first one. It was, apparently, just what Smith had schemed. He gave the ball a terrific ride into deep center field, but the nimble gardener out there brought it down after a long run.

"Off the bench, everybody! Let's go! Everybody alive now! Don't worry about that, Red, boy. We'll get you some runs next time! We'll get you a lead! Make 'em hit to me. . . . "

The short, stocky clean-up man who had been at bat for Hope when his teammate failed to steal second in the preceding inning came to bat. Warily, the Sonora team edged farther back.

But the batter crossed them up. After looking at Red's first pitch, a high one on the outside, he suddenly shifted and dumped a perfect bunt down the third-base line.

Red Bailey and Buck Losey both made a wild scramble for it. Red got there first, but by the time he checked his headlong run and whirled, it was obvious that the runner had him beaten. He held the ball and returned slowly to the mound.

Pretty slick, Bronc thought to himself out in right field. They're a hustling, smart little team, all right. But we'll get to their pitcher. He can't hold men like Chic Stahl and Smitty and Bill Burnham all day. They'll get to him in another inning or so. Then watch out! The rattle of base hits will sound like a machine gun. Our big job is up to Red Bailey. Red's got to hold 'em at the plate, or all the runs in the world can't win. Wonder where this gent is fixing to hit—swinging from the port-side, isn't he? All right, Mr. Lefty, just try to get one past out here!

The left-handed visitor did; a long single between Bronc and Bill Burnham in center. But Bronc stabbed it on the run, halted in his tracks, and shot a terrific strike to Buck Losey on third, which nailed the surprised clean-up man who had been on first when the ball was hit. And that wasn't all! From the corner of his eye, Buck Losey saw the other man attempting to take second on the play, and his quick peg erased him, too.

Two down! The sacks clear now. Again Red Bailey had things his own way.

As the game wore on, Sonora's superior hitting power began to take effect. By the ninth inning they had a comfortable ten-to-six lead, and although weakening noticeably, Red Bailey managed to stick to his job.

Bronc caught the last ball, a high fly that came to him almost without moving. He stuck it in his pocket, trotting back to the bench, as his noisy, eager teammates jabbered and howled like a wolf pack.

"That's the way to go, gang! We've got four wins now! Four and one, it is—and somebody will beat Spur! Then we'll be tied for first place! Wow! Wouldn't that be something: a championship for little Sonora! Shucks, nothing impossible about it! They can't beat us, because we won't let 'em—not if we keep hustling! But that's it: we've all gotta hustle. . . . "

Fat Crompton's big, sweaty face was all smiles as he walked off the diamond with Bronc, his arm around Bronc's shoulder. "You played a swell game, pal!" he babbled eagerly. "Your dad will be really tickled. Seven put-outs, three men cut off at the plate, and two hits—"

"Both scratches," Bronc interrupted soberly. "Neither one hard enough to break its way out of a paper sack."

"But they both scored runs! And those bullets you threw from the field— Wow! You'll have a mortgage on right, from here on!"

"That's what I'm afraid of."

"Say—" Fat halted, pulling Bronc to a stop, too.

Bronc did not wait for his pal to question him. "I've just been thinking," he said slowly. "A fellow's got to have a good 'change of pace' to get anywhere as a pitcher. Mine is punk, you can always tell ahead of time when I'm going to throw it. Why don't you come out to the ranch over the week end, and we'll practice."

"Now you're talking real sense!" Fat Crompton grinned delightedly. "I've said all the time that you're ninety-nine parts pitcher, and only one part outfielder!"

"Then you'll come?"

"Not tonight. I've got a whole flock of jobs around Dad's store. Can't put 'em off any longer, or he'll paddle my canoe. But I'll see you in the morning—sure—*Mr. Pitcher!*"

"Thanks for the kind words!"

Chapter 7

BASEBALL STRATEGY

"The use of signals," Cap'n Al Carter told his assembled protégés at their next practice session, "is one of the most important things in baseball. And it's fascinating, provided you're on the inside and know what's going on. Baseball history is packed with games that were won or lost by the 'tying of a shoestring,' or a 'hitch of the belt,' or a 'slap at a bug.' "

"I remember reading about that one!" Fibate Jones boasted. "It happened when the Cardinals were playing in Philadelphia one night."

"Yes. One night when the bugs were awfully bad the the Cardinals had a runner on third, with a long hitter at the plate, so their manager intended to give the hit-away signal. But, instead, at just the wrong time, a bug lit on the end of his nose. He slapped it off without thinking. Well, rubbing his nose was the Cardinal manager's signal for the runner to advance on the next pitch. The runner caught that signal and dashed for home plate. But the batter hadn't seen it! So instead of bunting, or trying for a hit to protect the runner, he just stood there while an outside ball plunked into the catcher's hands. The Philly catcher, of course, made an easy put-out of the runner coming in to him, and the Cardinal rally was squelched."

"I'll bet the crowd really hooted at that poor runner,"

Bronc Burnett said. "Not knowing about the mix-up in signals, they would probably figure he had pulled a bonehead play."

"You're always thinking about the crowd!" Fibate Jones scoffed acidly. "And what the crowd said! And how to answer them back! And—"

"That will do!" Cap'n Al broke in, frowning at Fibate.

"Aw, I don't mind, Coach!" Bronc grinned good-naturedly. "That rabbit ears stuff is as dead as a doornail."

"We've got too much baseball on the docket for today to be wasting any time at wrangling. I'm going to start with thirty minutes' instruction on signals, then we'll hustle through a regular practice."

The team was assembled on the grass in front of the backstop. Most of them were sitting with their backs against the wire, but toward first base Bronc Burnett lay sprawled at full length, between Fat Crompton and Pitch Carson. Out in front of them, his back to home plate and the diamond, Cap'n Al Carter was half leaning, half sitting, on the big end of an upturned baseball bat.

The day was warm; one of those still, clear spring days when baseball lives in the very air a healthy boy breathes. And today, like every other day when the former big leaguer was on hand, the Sonora youngsters were wide-eyed and alert. Each one of them had a ball, a bat, or a glove in his hand—attention glued on the forceful character just in front.

"Our situation in the Sapello Valley conference is considerably different from the professional leagues," Cap'n Al began. "Up there, each team plays each other team a couple of dozen times a season. As a result, they get mighty familiar with their opponents' style of play. They keep notes on the other fellows' strong points, their weaknesses, their signals, and so forth. While here, you'd almost call us strangers. We only play one another a single game.

"For that reason, I am not going to give you a complicated system. We'll not be trying to steal the other teams' signals, and we'll assume, in turn, that they will not be swiping ours.

"Now, I don't mean to imply that we'll make ours too obvious," he hastened to explain. "As a matter of fact, they will be 'professional.' But instead of having several different sets, we'll get by with just one. The big leagues always have three or four sets of signals, and may change sets every inning, or even *during* an inning, if they think their opponents are getting wise to their plays.

"For example: our signal to bunt will be the closed right fist. The closed right fist, then, means to bunt. Get that, everybody? Okay!

"Since we probably won't use this more than four or five times during a game, and with only one game against each team, I don't think we need worry about its being intercepted, especially if we keep doing other little mannerisms. Any one of them might be the real signal. However, if some team does get wise, I'll immediately teach you a new set. But until they do, I don't want to clutter your minds with too many things."

"Excuse me, sir," Bronc asked, as the coach paused momentarily for breath, "but what is the attitude toward stealing signals? Is it considered poor sportsmanship, or just good baseball?"

"It's both, depending on the circumstances. Some of the big teams, for instance, have gone so far as to plant their spies out in the center-field stands with telescopes. They read the catcher's signal to the pitcher, whether it's to be a fast ball, a curve, or a change of pace, then flash word to their batter. It gives the batter a tremendous advantage, of course, and they've knocked the socks off'n some very good pitchers just because they knew what was coming each time.

"In high school competition," Cap'n Al continued, "where we try to maintain the highest standards of ethics and all-round character building, such a practice would not be tolerated. I'd call that sort of signal stealing very poor sportsmanship.

"On the other hand, after five or six innings against some team, suppose we have observed that their signal to steal a base is for the coach to stand with both hands on his knees. All right, suppose now they have a runner on first. And when our catcher notices that they're planning to send the runner down to second, it would be, as you say, just good baseball for us to try to block the play. And in that case, the catcher should signal Bronc, or Pitch Carson—whoever happens to be on the mound for us at the time—to throw him a waste ball, outside, so he would be in good shape, without interference from the batter, to whip a fast peg to second."

Fat Crompton nudged Bronc with his elbow. But he needn't have! Bronc, too, had caught the full significance of Cap'n Al's words.

He was going to get another try on the mound! He was still a pitcher, despite his fine showing in the outfield the week before. Gee—that was wonderful! He couldn't help glancing sideways toward Fibate Jones. Fibate was scowling black as night. So Fibate had caught on, too! Well, that wouldn't make any difference, because—

Cap'n Al was speaking again: "Stealing another team's signals can be disastrous. We must not overlook that. Suppose they have a man or two on base, and you think they're going to bunt; suppose you've seen a coach mop his face with a handkerchief, stoop down and pick up a handful of dirt, or some other little mannerism, and you think the batter is being ordered to dump one. All right, as a result, you infielders come dashing in. Then suppose that isn't the play at all. See what would happen? You'd be wide open for any sort of hit ball—clear out of position—they'd probably ruin you. They might even hurt one of you, if you got caught in the face with a line smash as you came running in close.

"So unless you're dead sure of the play they're going to attempt, it's best not to go all out in trying to block it. The same thing holds true of trying to outguess a pitcher. If you guess wrong, you're apt to get hurt. For example: if you think he's going to throw a curve, and you get all set for one, then instead it's a fast ball inside, you stand a good chance of getting plunked in the ribs!"

"But how can a team steal signals from the pitcher?" Fat Crompton inquired. "Pitchers don't give signals. It's guys like me, the catchers, who call for each throw from the mound. And if the catcher is onto his job, his signal will be covered so the batter can't possibly see it. How could the *pitcher* give it away?"

Cap'n Al grinned. "Lots of ways!" he chuckled. "Perhaps the most famous case was Babe Ruth. The Babe used to be a pitcher for Boston in his early days. A mighty good pitcher, too. But unknown even to himself, he developed a habit of sticking out his tongue each time he got ready to throw a curve. Word went around the league in no time. And how they used to fatten their batting averages against him, until a player whom they had got in a trade from another team tipped him off!

"They say Ed Walsh, of the Chicago White Sox, used to touch his cap unconsciously when he got ready to throw a spitball. And George Smith always gave off a tip by the expression in his eyes: for a fast ball they'd get big and wide like an owl's, and for his spitter they would narrow down to a couple of tiny slits. Does that answer your question?"

"Perfectly!" Fat grinned. "It means we'll have to pound a little sense into these dumb pitchers of our own!"

"And the catchers, too!"

"Aw, what do you mean, sir?"

"Well, let's start with you; you're quite a good tipper-offer yourself, Crompton. I noticed the other day when you and Bronc were warming up, every time you signaled for a fast ball, you came up out of your crouch by putting both hands on your thighs. When you called for a curve, you straightened up directly, with your arms extended. And when—now, hold on!" Cap'n Al cautioned, as Fat seemed about to interrupt. "Don't argue that the batter wouldn't be able to see how you rose to your feet. A smart batter would! But even if he didn't, there's another way he could tell what *you* had signaled for, and he wouldn't even have to look back out of the corner of his eye.

"Here's what I mean: Every time you called for a fast one, your chatter was, 'Okay in there, Bronc! Shove it in here, boy!' And each time you called for a curve, you'd say, 'Come on with 'er, Bronc! Shove it across here, old boy!' See what I mean?"

Cap'n Al flashed a grin at Crompton, now bulgy-eyed, his jaw sagging open.

A chorus of chuckles swept the rest of the team.

"Oh, Crompton isn't the only tipper-offer!" Cap'n Al hastened to inform them. "You're all offenders. Let's take you, Bill Burnham, for another horrible example—clear out there in center field, innocently minding your own business, eh? Well, here's what I noticed: You could see the catcher's signals, couldn't you? Of course! Well, each time he called for a curve on a right-handed batter, I saw you take two steps to your right; and each time he called for a fast one, you'd move two steps to your left. That's good baseball—it means you're using your head—anticipating a slower or faster swing by the batter. But you should wait until the pitch is delivered! Otherwise, by watching you, a batter would know ahead of time just what our poor pitcher was going to throw. They'd blast him out of his shoes!"

"I'll watch my step—my *steps*, rather—from now on, sir!" Bill Burnham promised. "Gosh! There's an awful lot to baseball that the ordinary spectator never knows about."

"Right! And I've only just started to tell you. But let's get back briefly to our signals between the catcher and pitcher.

"The standard catcher's signal, with no hostile runners on base," Cap'n Al explained, "is pretty much the same everywhere in baseball: one finger for a fast ball, two for a curve, and three for a change of pace. Usually for a waste ball—one purposely wide of the plate, so the catcher can grab it for a quick peg to a base—it's the closed fist. Don't get this mixed with our signal to bunt, which is going to be the closed fist. I'm talking now of the private signals between the pitcher and the catcher, when we're in the field rather than at bat. Is that clear to you all? Okay!

"Now, if a chucker happens to disagree with his catcher's selection of a pitch, he just shakes his head. Usually, the catcher will then call for something else. However, if the catcher is dead sure that he is right, and has some particular reason for calling the pitch, he'll probably walk out to the mound, for a little conference. It's a teamwork proposition, after all, and they both should have a share in the decisions on how to pitch to each batter."

"But who's supreme?" Fibate Jones wanted to know. "Suppose the catcher insists on a fast one, and the pitcher is just as determined to give him a curve—who takes priority?"

"Neither one, on my team!" Cap'n Al replied, a trifle curtly. "My pitchers and catchers must be close friends, because no ball club is going to get anywhere with a chucker and his catcher at odds. I won't stand for any such bullheadedness.

"Of course, there will always be the human element to consider, and a catcher must take that into account when calling his signals. Even if a batter is known to be weak against a change of pace, a catcher shouldn't ask his battery mate to throw one if the pitcher just isn't effective with his. Or, the catcher may know that a certain batter is a sucker for a low, outside curve ball, but perhaps his pitcher can't control his curve that accurately; in that case, especially on a three-two pitch, he wouldn't dare risk it, even though with some other pitcher on the mound it would be the logical throw.

"Then there will be circumstances when a catcher will apparently be calling for a pitch right to a man's strength. It's done in the big leagues every day. A dozen times a day! A certain batter, for instance, under normal conditions will hit a fly to right field if given a fast one over the inside corner. Okay—plant your fielders handily, and give it to him—especially if you're leading by a comfortable margin and want to conserve a pitcher's strength. It makes a lot of difference, over the nine-inning route, if a chucker can get by with only two or three pitches to a batter, instead of five or six. Then he'll have the reserve strength to really bear down if he does get into a pinch.

"But let's get back to our signals!" Cap'n Al said hastily. "I'll take up the pitching chores directly with Carson and Lear and Burnett and Bailey; no use bothering the rest of you with their headaches."

"We're just drinking it up, sir!" Fat Crompton protested.

"You'd better be—you're a catcher!"

"It's flattery, calling him a catcher!" Fibate Jones muttered to those nearest him. "If you ask me—"

That was as far as he got. Fat Crompton's big hand clamped itself over his mouth, hauled him sideways off of balance. Cap'n Al noted the move, started to intercede, then noticed the broad grin on Crompton's face.

"The only time you'll need to vary the catcher-pitcher signals from the one-two-three fingers I mentioned is with a runner on second base. In that event, the runner may start tipping off the batter; the runner can see them from second, you know."

Bronc Burnett held up his hand. "But couldn't we hear him—and change?"

"A smart base runner doesn't call out openly. He'd disguise it so you would never suspect. Left hand on his belt, for instance, might mean a curve was coming. Right hand on the belt, a fast one. Or, he might even have a prearranged verbal code. Any sentence containing the word 'base' might mean to look out for a curve: 'Give us a base hit, boy!' Or, 'Get on base, old fellow!' And so on. Then, perhaps a sentence containing the word 'pill' might mean the fast ball: 'Come on! Sock the old pill, fellow!' Or, 'Give the old pill a ride, boy!' You see, there are lots of ways to communicate, and still keep it disguised.

"However," Cap'n Al corrected himself again, "here we've strayed over into the battery's private pasture again! No more of that for today. I want to take up our offensive signals now, the signals we will use when we're at bat.

"In high school baseball, it isn't generally considered good taste for an adult to be too conspicuous during a game, the emphasis nowadays being to let the boys themselves make more and more of the decisions. So I'm going to be a 'bench manager.' Starting with our game next Friday at Mesquite, we'll have two of you regularly assigned for the coaching jobs at first and third bases. I'll call the set plays, of course, while the two base coaches will handle the runners on all emergencies.

"You," Cap'n Al said, indicating Lefty Lear, "will handle first base—always—except when you're pitching. And you, Trail—" pointing to the team's canny, little shortstop, "will be our coach at third. When you're at bat or running bases yourself, I'll appoint somebody else for the time being.

"Now, don't think this is punishment, or in the nature

of extra duty. Actually, it is an honor to both of you boys.

"An alert base coach, able to size up situations and make good, quick decisions on the spur of the moment, is positively worth his weight in gold baseballs. It isn't the kind of a job for a chess-playing type of mind, or for a methodical professor; it's a thing that calls for split-second, snap judgment. It will take courage. The courage to gamble if conditions seem to justify it. At the same time, it also calls for a mass of informative background.

"I want you to become thoroughly familiar with our team's abilities, individually—to know who is fast, who can slide well. And, vice versa, who can't do these things well. This knowledge is extremely important because it will influence your decisions—whether to send a fast runner on for an extra base when the ball is in play, or to hold a slower one safe. It's out of my hands then—onto your shoulders.

"You'll have to study the opposing teams, too, but I'll help you with that. We'll learn which outfielders have the best throwing arms—like Bronc's here—men who are able to nail a runner at the plate from way back in the field. Have to play safe, then. Can't take any liberties when the ball is hit to a man like Bronc, as he showed Hope last Friday. And again, vice versa, we'll know about it if any of the opposing outfielders have weak throwing arms. You'll take longer risks against them and send runners on for extra bases. Now, so far, are there any questions?"

The little group stayed hushed momentarily, every eye remaining on Cap'n Al. Then Fat Crompton's hand went up.

"Do I gather," he asked, "that you are planning to keep Bronc Burnett in the outfield?"

A quick flush spread through the coach's strong features, and for the barest instant his jaws clamped rigidly

93

together. But his sunny nature quickly broke the surface again.

"That question," he replied, throwing Fat a grin that wasn't unfriendly, "comes under the heading of my own private business! Besides, it has nothing to do with our use of signals. Now, any more questions?"

There were none, apparently.

"You shouldn't have done that, you old buzzard!" Bronc Burnett whispered to his pal. "I'm going to play my head off for Cap'n Al, no matter where he puts me!"

"But it may cost us the Valley championship if he doesn't put you on the mound where you belong. And you'd far rather pitch, wouldn't you? But you needn't answer that," Crompton added. "It shows in your face! And the team needs—"

"Sh-h-h! Here come the signals!"

"As I mentioned," Cap'n Al continued, "our signal for the bunt will be the closed fist. My closed fist—right hand. Get that, everybody? All right, now for the steal signal: it will be for either hand to stroke the opposite armpit. Like this!" He reached across his chest with his right hand, briefly rubbing a spot beneath his left arm. "Or, this!" He reversed the motion. "Get that, everybody—that's for the steal! Now for the hit-away—that means for a batter to use his own judgment. Hit, if the pitch is in there. Let it go if it isn't. Our signal for the hit-away will be my cap tilted back on my head. Like this!" Again he showed them.

"For the present, I'll only give you one more; our signal for the batter to let a pitch go past. 'Taking a pitch,' we call it, meaning not to strike, no matter how fat it looks. All right, when I want you to take the next pitch, I'll place one hand behind my neck. Either hand behind my neck, you see? Are there any questions?"

"There's just one thing," Trail Drover suggested. "Sometimes the crowd gets in the way, or a player walks in front of you at the wrong time. In a case like that

94

—say, with one of us as a runner on second—we might fail to catch your signal."

"An excellent point!" the coach said, with a smile of encouragement. "That's using your head! All right, here's what we do: Any time you fail to catch the signal, you promptly bend over and fidget with your garter for a moment. We'll be watching, and we'll repeat the signal. Keep fidgeting with your garter until you know exactly what the signal is.

"However, that brings up another point that will answer your question, too: None of you fellows, either at bat, or running the bases, will take any signals from me directly. You'll get them from the coaches at first and third who will relay my signals. That way, you'll always have a man easy to find and to watch. Get 'em from *him*—not me! It will make it particularly easy for the batters. A left-handed batter, who naturally faces third base when he's at the plate, will merely glance at the coach on third for his signal. A right-hand hitter, reversely, will take his signals from the coach on first before each pitched ball. The coaches, with less on their minds and not being under the strain of immediate competition, will have more leisure and opportunity to get the signals from me, to pass on. And never stand and gawk for your signal! Get it at a glance, then keep your eyes some place else. Don't make a coach continue holding the signal any longer than is absolutely necessary.

"One last thing I want to mention," Cap'n Al concluded. "Very often we'll use two signals at once, a combination of signals, that is. So be sure you don't go to sleep on that! Suppose I do this . . ." He rubbed one hand across the back of his neck with seeming carelessness, meanwhile half supporting the upraised arm with his opposite hand, which hovered in the vicinity of his armpit. It wasn't a stilted position at all, nor one that was particularly conspicuous. "What does that mean?"

Instantly Trail Drover's hand went up.

"All right, Trail!"

"It means for the batter to let a pitch go past, and for the runner to steal!"

"Good stuff, boy! Now, we'll get out on the field and start limbering up. I'm going to work the living daylights out of you all today! We'll have a wildcat by the tail in Friday's game. Mesquite has beaten Vocant and Suerte, both by larger scores than we did, and they'll be playing on their home pasture besides. We'll have to hit. We'll have to be smart. And we'll have to hustle, or there won't be any championship pie for Sonora this year! Now, get moving, all of you!"

That became the hardest, longest practice of the season thus far, and there wasn't a single member of the team with any spring left in his stride, as they dragged themselves laboriously to the dressing room afterward.

Fat Crompton was the first to flop onto a bench, but he still had vim enough to pull Bronc down beside him when his buddy entered the room. "Well—what *are* you?" He panted exhaustedly. "Are you a pitcher, or an outfielder?"

Bronc Burnett's powerful young shoulders had sagged wearily, but he could still grin through his dust and sweat.

Slowly he shook his head. "Search me! He had me pitching until I was blue in the face, but then I batted, too, and I also shagged a million flies. Your guess is as good as mine!"

Chapter 8

TWO ARE SUSPENDED

THE team was ready for Mesquite on Friday. Everybody was sure of it; that is, everybody but Cap'n Al Carter. And Cap'n Al didn't count. "Automatically disqualified!" one wag put it, because he was the coach. Coaches were always pessimistic. Couldn't please a coach, even if his team was perfect! Why, anybody could see this gang was good. They were a dozen runs better than when Spur had lifted their scalps.

And it was true, there were grounds for optimism. Never in the history of Sonora, either high school or independent, had any team shown half the all-round class of this present aggregation.

Their hitting, not by any means bad before, had now progressed to the point of sheer viciousness. Even little Peedink Harrell had got the knack of pounding short line drives just beyond the infield; while the team's two sluggers, Bill Burnham and "Slow Molasses" Smith, were averaging ten to fifteen yards' extra distance in their clouting. Endless coaching on how to improve their stances at the plate, more rhythmical swings, and the natural results of spirited long practice sessions had paid excellent dividends.

Defensively, the improvement was just as marked. By following Cap'n Al's advice on how to pivot, how to whip throws away faster, and how to co-ordinate their play one with another, the infield now fairly sparkled with speed and confidence.

"But don't get too swelled on yourselves!" the coach kept warning them sourly. "Remember, Mesquite is working hard, too, and they'll be improving. While a big-league team may often slip backward and lose its co-ordination through age or other reasons, a high school team always improves. They're young. They're learning. So don't get any cockeyed ideas that Mesquite is going to be standing still, or getting worse, while you're getting better!"

The team and their schoolmates always listened respectfully to this. Nor did any of them venture to argue with the veteran. But in their youthful enthusiasm over the miracle he had worked with them in such a short time, they simply couldn't believe that other teams would have been so blessed. The two-foot silver and gold championship trophy was as good as delivered already!

Meanwhile, Bronc Burnett still didn't know just where he stood in the coach's plans. Daily throughout the rest of the week, as on Monday, he had dabbled in all phases of the game, though it did seem that Cap'n Al was keeping him on the mound longer than all of the other hurling aspirants combined. Several times, however, the coach had to call him down severely for throwing too hard.

"Remember, it's batting practice for the team, not pitching practice for you! And no curves, either! I want to develop confidence, above everything else, in these hitters. I want them to be *eager* to get to the plate, not *scared!* So save your fancy stuff for pitching practice to Crompton!"

"I'll try, sir!"

But Nature had endowed Bronc Burnett with a fast ball that was terrifically fast; and frequently he didn't realize just how much smoke he was getting into a pitch. Then too, Bronc was young, still a boy, subject to a boy's natural impulses and temptations. So in spite of himself and his unquestioned loyalty to Cap'n Al, it was only natural that he should cut loose with an occasional fireball that would leave some batter gaping open-mouthed. Then maybe he would follow with the same pitching motion again, threatening another fast one, only to cross his man with a tantalizing "floater"—the change of pace he had practiced with Crompton. But most of the time, however, he would groove every pitch fast enough to hit well and not so fast as to be difficult. And just as Cap'n Al had intended, the hitters came to love their turns at the plate with Bronc on the mound.

Pitch Carson seemed to have regained his old form, and if the injured hand bothered him at all it was seldom in evidence because his control was good; and in private practice Drake Yoder claimed his stuff was as sharp as ever. He had kept himself in condition all the while his hand was bandaged, so his come-back efforts had been largely a matter of getting his arm in shape.

"I believe he's ready to go," Bronc heard Drake, the regular catcher, tell Cap'n Al on the night before they left for Mesquite.

"So am I!" Bronc grunted to himself.

As it was only seventeen miles down the canyon to Mesquite, the team attended all morning classes and remained for lunch at Sonora on the day of the game. The entire student body and several dozen well-wishers from town were on hand to wave a noisy, hopeful "Good luck!" as they climbed into the bus.

Cap'n Al had all four of his pitchers warming up at least half an hour before game time. And not until the last minute did he indicate which would draw the starting assignment. Then:

"Get your sweater on, Burnett! Go over to the bench and sit down, and be sure you keep that salary arm covered!"

"Then you're starting me? Gee! That's—"

"No, I'm starting Carson. You'll play right field, but I want you to take care of that arm."

"Yes, sir!"

Bronc turned and slowly walked to the bench, where he untangled his sweater from a mass of others and put it on. Fat Crompton slid down beside him. Fat was sweating profusely, and open rebellion showed in his big features, but he kept his words to himself.

A burly, square-jawed man, wearing a blue flannel shirt and blue pants, walked out to home plate. He had a chest protector slung over one arm and was carrying a mask in one hand and a glistening white ball in the other. With a quick look around to see that everything was in readiness, he glanced down at his penciled notes on the baseball.

"Batteries for today's game!" he announced. "For Sonora: Carson, pitching; Yoder, catching. For Mesquite: Pilar and Burch! Play ball!"

The home team sprinted onto the diamond. They were a peppery lot, larger than the average high school team, and seemingly well coached. The crowd up in the big grandstand, since Mesquite had a completely fenced park, gave them tremendous encouragement as they passed the ball expertly around. Their pitcher, Pilar, was a tall, rangy fellow with long arms and an easy-looking throw. His face was dark, swarthy, and had the set, mature lines of a man rather than a youth in his teens.

Trail Drover was already at his post on the third-base coaching line for Sonora, and Lefty Lear, heavily sweatered, had gone out to first. Both boys stood studying the Mesquite final warmup, and almost as if their thoughts could have been heard, it was obvious to their teammates on the bench that they were eagerly hawking their opponents for any of the weaknesses their coach had described.

"Play ball!"

Peedink Harrell stepped to the plate. Over on the

Sonora bench Cap'n Al Carter tilted his cap back on his head. Quick as a wink, almost, Lefty Lear and Trail Drover did the same, meanwhile clapping their hands and walking restlessly back and forth. Peedink had glanced at Lear momentarily, then turned full attention to the pitcher. It was apparent that Peedink understood. Had his wits about him, all right. Getting to be a good lead-off man. Was ready, now, for the hit-away, to use his own judgment.

Strike one—called! The crowd yelled delightedly.

"Come on, Peedink!" Lefty Lear yelled from first, between cupped hands. "Want to see you down here, boy!"

Ball one. Ball two. Then, ball three! The crowd hushed uneasily. Then, strike two! That was better; a chorus of cheers urged the pitcher on. Pilar wound up deliberately, turned loose a fast ball.

Peedink swung, connected. The ball zipped on a line just above the first baseman's reach, for a clean single into right. Lefty Lear watched the right fielder keenly, saw him scoop up the ball and instantly fire it to second, so he held Peedink at first. Chic Stahl was up. Instantly Cap'n Al brushed his right hand across the back of his neck. The two coaches repeated the motion; the signal not to swing at the first one.

At the plate Chic Stahl brandished his bat menacingly as if he couldn't wait to get into action. But when Pilar threw, he made no attempt whatever to strike, even though the pitch had been good. The Mesquite infield, obviously expecting a bunt, had come racing inside the base lines.

Cap'n Al now held up his right fist. For the barest instant Lefty Lear did the same, just enough to realize that Chic had seen. Then he resumed his restless pacing up and down the coaching box, now calling encouragement to Peedink on first near by, and now yelling for a home run from Chic over at the plate.

But Chic wasn't bent on any home run, though his stance and long-handled grip did indicate it. Instead, at the last split second he shifted his feet and hands and tipped a beautiful bunt down the third-base line. This time the team hadn't come in, apparently bluffed by his hitter stance, and they just couldn't get to the ball quick enough. Pilar and the third baseman both made a try, but the nimble-footed Chic was within easy distance of first before Pilar picked up the ball, so Pilar didn't risk a throw. Peedink Harrell, of course, had made second on the play. Two on; nobody down! Pilar plunked the ball savagely into his glove a dozen times as he strode back to the mound.

"Slow Molasses" Smith came to bat.

Hit-away.

Smitty didn't waste any time. He promptly stepped into the very first pitched ball, swinging from his heels. It was not a center blow, else it would have cleared the fence, but it was solidly enough hit that it sent their right fielder backpedaling furiously before he pulled it down. Meanwhile, Trail Drover, coaching for Sonora at third, was on the alert and yelled Peedink into advancing from second to third after the catch. The Mesquite right fielder made a try for him—it was close—but Peedink slid under the throw. And the instant he had seen them try for Peedink at third, Lefty Lear had spurred Chic Stahl on to second. Safe all the way around! The coaches were doing a heads-up job.

Runners camped on second and third now. Only one down! Even a single would score two runs. A grounder, or a fly, would bring in one!

Bill Burnham, clean-up man and heaviest slugger on the Sonora team, came to the plate. Bill wore a grin a yard wide as he rubbed one sleeve across his forehead, and then stood brandishing his huge war club.

Out on the mound Pilar shook his head at some signal the catcher had called. Then he shook it again. The Mesquite catcher walked out to talk with him. Presently he was back. Their strategy was quickly obvious.

Ball one. Ball two. Ball three. Ball *four!*

"They walked him on purpose!" Bronc Burnett gasped in amazement. "They deliberately walked the bases full!"

"Sure! With one out, it's sometimes good baseball," Cap'n Al explained. "They're going to try for a double-play ball on Buck, our next hitter. See . . . Their infielders haven't come in closer? They're going to play deep and hope for a grounder that would lead to a twin killing. It's a gamble, of course, but a good team will succeed oftener than they fail. That's what we call playing percentage ball. Well, let's see what happens!"

He gave the signal for Buck Losey to hit-away.

As a result of his showing the week before, Bronc had been elevated a notch in the batting order, and he would follow Buck; so he picked out his bat now and hurried to the chalked ring, crouching on one knee to watch.

The first pitch to Buck Losey was a ball . . . outside. Then on the next one, a fast ball, Buck hit a long foul down the first-base line. One and one, now. Bases still full, their infield still playing deep.

Suddenly Bronc caught his breath. The signal—he saw that Cap'n Al was calling for a bunt. Something would happen now. It had to! Bases full, only one out, and Buck Losey getting ready to dump a sleeper. Bronc saw the Mesquite pitcher, deadly serious now, step methodically onto the rubber slab. With a last careful check of the runners, Pilar took a half windup, then threw.

It was an inside, high, fast ball—the hardest possible ball to bunt. But Buck Losey tried gamely. He met the ball, all right, but his aim was poor, and it popped straight out in front of him, about twenty or thirty feet high. Pilar made the catch, then whirled for a savage peg to third. Too late—by an eyelash! Peedink Harrell had been halfway home when the pop-up occurred, and only the slow, lazy flight of the ball had enabled him to scamper back to base ahead of Pilar's catch and throw.

Two down now. Bases still full. Bedlam broke loose up in the crowded stands, as Bronc Burnett walked into the batter's box. He noted his signal: the hit-away. Good!

Bronc may have looked relaxed and nonchalant, but actually his heart was pounding like the base drum in a military march. Bases full . . . they might not get another chance like this! The game might depend on what he did right now. Well, anyhow, his mind was made up on one thing: They'd never call him out on strikes! He was up here to hit! And he was going to hit!

It must have shown in his manner. At any rate, the first pitch was a low, sweeping curve outside. Too late, Bronc saw that it was in the dirt, but he had already started his swing. Strike one! The home crowd yelled delightedly, because Bronc had looked bad on that pitch. Might get out of this hole, after all! Good boy, Pilar, throw another one past him!

Again Bronc and the Mesquite pitcher faced each other.

You made a sucker out of me that time, Bronc thought grimly, but you can't do it again! Just try me on another curve, and I'll show you! It's got to be in here, or I won't—

Here came the pitch—starting for the same outside corner. Bronc let it go. But the ball didn't break as the first one had. It had streaked across the corner—fast.

Strike two! Bronc bit his lip, as beads of perspiration stood out on his square, sandy features. He still had one left. It only took one.

"Come on, boy!" Lefty Lear begged from the first-base coaching line. "I want to see you down here! Give us a base knock, boy!"

Bronc managed to put temptation aside sufficiently to let two more sweeping curves dart past him, far wide of the plate. Two and two now—that was better. But the next one would be across. You could bet your shirt on that! With the bases loaded, and a supposedly weak hitter at bat, Pilar wouldn't waste another pitch. He'd shove it across. Well, let 'er come!

The pitch was fast, closer inside than Bronc would have liked, but he dared not take a chance on it being called against him, so he swung. Bat hit ball squarely. It felt good. But, shucks! There it went straight toward second, looping along with "handles" on it!

Nevertheless, Bronc tore out for first. "Run everything the limit!" the coach had told them repeatedly. "The other fellow might fumble, or your own hustling action might hurry him into a wild peg—so run!" But even though Bronc dashed down the base line with the speed of a scared antelope, the ball was there ahead of him.

Three outs! Nobody had scored—after filling the bases! The crowd roared with a gusto that fairly rocked the grandstand.

Bronc trotted back toward the Sonora bench for his glove.

He was met halfway by Fat Crompton, who tossed it to him. "Tough luck, pardner! But, doggone it, you ought to be on the hill instead of right field!"

"Thanks, Fat! There'll be other times."

Bronc turned and raced for his post. Bill Burnham and Peedink Harrell were already tossing balls to each other, and as Bronc reached position Bill threw a looping toss to him. Meanwhile, the infield was passing their practice ball back and forth, and Pitch Carson was making his five allowable throws to Drake Yoder at the plate.

"Batter up—play ball!"

A slim, crouching little left-hander came to bat for Mesquite. Instantly a flood of chatter broke from the Sonora team afield:

"Let's hold 'em, gang! Everybody alive out here now!

What do you say in there, Pitch? Make him hit to me, boy! . . ."

Pitch Carson's first throw was so wide of the plate that Drake Yoder had to dive headlong to stop it. Slowly he picked himself up, walked out in front of the plate several steps, then tossed it back.

"Steady in there, Pitch!" Bronc heard him call through his mask. "This guy isn't tough. Just settle down now, and pitch ball!"

The next attempt was better; a called strike. But as Pitch Carson turned loose another, the batter teed off against him. *Crack!* Bronc, out in right field, instinctively leaned forward, then saw it was well enough hit to reach him. He stood perfectly still. Without making a move forward or back, nor to the right or left, he simply held up his hands and let the ball come to him. He fired it into Smith on first with a whip that nearly lifted the big fellow off of his feet.

"Hey, you monkey!" Smith protested. "Do you think I've got a feather mattress on my hand?"

Bronc grinned, with a careless wave.

"All right, let's get number two! Make him hit to Bronc. Bronc's got the old eagle eye out there! On your toes, everybody. . . ."

The second Mesquite batter, however, a gangling left-hander, pounded Pitch's first throw for a terrific hit between Bronc and Bill Burnham. Both gave frantic chase. The ball struck the fence in deep center and bounded back, high. It looked for a moment as if they had both run under it, but Bronc's desperate leap into the air speared it with one hand. He whirled, whipping the ball savagely to third. It was a marvelous throw, and in plenty of time to nail the runner too, but when the dust had cleared, the umpire was signaling "Safe!" Then Bronc saw the reason: Buck Losey had untangled him-self from the runner and was walking over to one side, where he picked up the ball. Disgustedly he pounded it into his glove, then tossed it back to the pitcher.

A runner on third! Only one down! The crowd was on its feet, begging for a hit.

Bronc noted that his teammates were playing close in on the grass. Looking for a bunt, obviously. But would Mesquite bunt? Was it logical, with their third-place hitter at the plate? The safest, best hitter on a team, according to Cap'n Al's teaching. Would they waste him on a play for just one run this early in the game? Evidently Cap'n Al figured they would, else he would have motioned his team back.

"Strike one!" The batter had not even taken the bat from his shoulder.

The Sonora infield stayed close. Still looking for a bunt! Bronc waited uneasily. Pitch Carson was back on the mound. The stretch . . . the throw . . . There! Sure enough, a bunt down the third-base line!

Pitch Carson and Buck Losey raced for the ball. Pitch got there first, scooped it up. But as he started to whirl, somehow his feet slipped, and he sat down flat on his rump. Not only did the runner score, but the batsman had reached first and now broke for second. Pitch got to his feet in time to have cut him off, but his throw was wide and the runner easily safe.

"Whew!" Bronc muttered worriedly. "That isn't like Pitch! This two weeks' layoff has sure hurt!"

A runner on second now. Scoring position. And only one down, as a buffalo-shouldered clean-up man stood ready to do murder at the plate. Gee, wouldn't they ever run out of left-handers? Each time this big brute took a practice swing, his bat seemed to threaten a sure hit into Bronc's territory.

Bronc noticed momentary activity on the Sonora bench, then saw Lefty Lear and Fat Crompton coming down the side lines. Fat had his catcher's mitt, and Lefty carried a warmup ball in his glove. They began to throw.

The big clean-up man smashed Pitch's first ball straight at Smith on first. Smith knocked it down, picked it up, then managed to beat the slow-running slugger to base. Two down, but the runner on second had taken third on the play. Mesquite still threatened.

Bronc observed that Lefty Lear was putting more and more steam into his throws to Crompton along the side line.

Out on the mound the Sonora infielders had gathered around Pitch Carson. Bronc guessed the reason: stalling! Stalling to let Pitch regain his breath, his composure. Probably they weren't even talking about baseball!

Presently, as if on signal, the infielders turned and ran to their positions. Drake Yoder tarried an instant longer than the rest, pressed a ball into Pitch's glove, slapped him on the back, and returned to the plate. The break seemed to have helped Pitch. At any rate, he fired two consecutive strikes across the platter, then forced the batsman to tap weakly to Chic Stahl on second. Chic tossed him out with ease. Sonora raced for the bench.

"Now, let's get us some runs, gang! Who's up first? Who's on deck? Come on, Trail! Save us all a turn, boy. . . ."

Buck Losey took Trail Drover's place in the coaching box at third, and Smith took Lefty Lear's at first. Lefty continued to warm up, though tossing slowly and easily now.

The Sonora half of that inning was a freak. Only three pitched balls! Trail Drover hit the first pitch, a long fly to center field; Drake, the big catcher, clouted the next to right; and Pitch Carson ended the abbreviated session by popping a high foul, which the first baseman easily caught about halfway to home plate.

How the crowd yelled and stamped! That was saving

energy! That was playing ball! Now, get some runs yourselves, boys—get a bigger, safer lead!

They started in to do just that. Pitch Carson hit the first batter, giving him a free ticket to first, and the second popped a short Texas Leaguer into left, which Peedink Harrell couldn't quite reach. The lead runner took third—runners on first and third now—nobody down.

"Come on in there, Pitch! We're all behind you, boy! Never mind that! Make 'em hit to me. . . ."

Pitch tightened momentarily, to the extent of getting two strikes past the following batter, though meanwhile the man on first had stolen second. It was an awkward spot—runners on second and third, with nobody down. Bronc half expected Cap'n Al to order a new pitcher onto the mound, but no such indication was forthcoming. Evidently he figured they were far enough down the batting list to be past the more dangerous hitters.

This current batsman, still another of Mesquite's endless left-handers, drove two long fouls down the first-base line, then straightened out a high fly to Bronc Burnett. Bronc made the put-out. And knowing the runner at third would tag up after the catch, then break for the plate, he instantly shot the ball home with everything he had behind it. It was more like a rifle shot than a throw—straight on a line to a spot about thirty feet in front of the waiting catcher, then plunk into his mitt on the first hop, just as the speeding runner attempted to bump him away from the plate. But Drake Yoder was baseball wise, and he was big. The runner, out by a wide margin, limped off to the bench, while Drake yelled new encouragement to his pitcher.

"That's two down, boy! That's getting out of the hole! Now, let's start working on number three. . . ."

There was still a runner on third, however, and a clean single over shortstop now scored him. The following batter fanned.

Two to nothing against them as Sonora came in to bat.

"I've just heard some interesting news, boys," Cap'n Al announced, as they huddled momentarily near the bench. "Suerte is leading Spur three to nothing at the end of the fifth! Does that mean anything to you?"

"Mean anything? Come on now, gang! Let's give everything we've got! We're gonna be tied for first. Spur is gonna lose! Wow! Let's hit Pilar with everything but the water bucket this inning! Who's up? Come on, Peedink! Let's get a lead. . . ."

Either the news that their arch rival was losing at last, or the fact that they had all been hitting in hard luck, anyhow, turned that inning into a rout. Eleven runs crossed the plate before the side was retired!

Sonora continued to fare well until the last of the seventh inning—that is, they made six more runs and played errorless ball, despite the way Pitch Carson had kept them almost constantly in hot water. Mesquite had managed to tally five more times, and might have scored a dozen, except for some particularly fancy fielding and throwing by Bronc Burnett.

But in the seventh, Cap'n Al called the floundering Pitch Carson to the bench. With two out, Pitch had walked three men in a row, so when the big clean-up man strode to the plate for Mesquite, Cap'n Al motioned Lefty Lear to the mound.

Lefty promptly came through. He set the big slugger down on strikes.

Seventeen to seven now. First of the eighth. Bronc had flied out to end the inning before, so Trail Drover was first hitter. He went to the box eagerly.

Meanwhile, Fat Crompton slid over beside Cap'n Al on the bench. "Coach," he said, "maybe I'm out of order, but you're trying to teach us smart baseball, aren't you? Well, do you mind if I ask a question?"

"Why, no. What's on your mind, Crompton?"

Fat swallowed, seeming to bolster his nerve. Then he

shifted sideways, looking the coach straight in the eye.

"I want to know," he demanded, "why you're keeping the best baseball pitcher in New Mexico off'n the mound? Why, neither Lefty Lear nor Pitch Carson either is good enough even to carry Bronc Burnett's glove! Now, I'm not saying you hold a grudge, but—"

Bronc reached over, caught Fat Crompton by the sleeve, attempted to pull him away. "That's none of our affair, Fat! Cap'n Al knows what he's doing! And I'm not complaining!"

"But I am!" Fat shoved Bronc away. He was already committed now, and there was no stopping him. "It's a downright shame, the way you're treating—"

Cap'n Al Carter turned. He was smiling, but it was a cold, cutting sort of smile, more like the snarl of a wolf. "You go to the dressing room!" he ordered Fat. "And get started right now!"

There was a moment's tense silence. Then:

"I reckon I'll go with him!" said Bronc Burnett.

"As you wish!"

The two got up, stepped back over the bench, and started for the gate.

"Good riddance," they heard Fibate Jones sneer, as they left the field.

Chapter 9

MASTER VS. PUPIL

"Is everybody here?" Cap'n Al asked the next Monday afternoon, as he approached the group of boys sprawled on the grass in front of the practice field backstop. He wore his usual sweat shirt, long-billed blue cap, and a new pair of spikes.

"Yes, sir!" Fibate Jones replied. "And two extra."

"What do you mean?"

"The two former players whom you suspended last Friday. They didn't seem to take the hint."

A quick frown clouded the coach's face. "Fibate," he said, "sometimes I think you're low-down enough to eat off the same plate with a snake! Now, let those boys alone, or—"

"That doesn't matter, Cap'n Al!" Bronc Burnett interrupted hastily. "I'm so cured of my rabbit ears that I couldn't hear a jackass bray inside a tin barn."

"A matter of listening to himself!" muttered Fibate.

The words were scarcely above a whisper, but Bronc heard. Hot blood rushed up to crimson his cheeks and neck, but otherwise he kept himself in hand. His eyes stayed on Cap'n Al Carter.

What would the coach do? Would he and Fat get to stay with the team? Or would—

"Did you notice," Fat Crompton whispered to Bronc, "that nobody snickered today at Fibate's jokes?"

"They will—later. He'll change tactics. Fibate's slippery as a greased fish."

"That isn't exactly what I meant. It seems—well, it seems like maybe the boys are on our side—like, maybe, they don't feel so bad toward us after all. Anyhow . . ."

Cap'n Al motioned for silence. Selecting a bat for his customary half-leaning, half-sitting position in front of the group, he drew a small notebook from his hip pocket.

"I've jotted down a few of the mistakes you made in Friday's twenty-one-to-nine win over Mesquite," he began. "It would take a page the size of a saddle blanket to hold them all!"

The team sat motionless as the former big-league star rehashed the preceding game from beginning to end. It wasn't all critical, however. Half a dozen of them came in for scattered bits of praise interspersed with the "bad." Only one player escaped mention—Bronc Burnett. But Bronc was as completely ignored as though he had never existed—no comment whatever on any of his fielding, which should have been labeled "brilliant" in anybody's notebook, and not even a reprimand for a "bonehead" he had pulled in the fifth inning, when he attempted to steal second with the bases full!

"I don't suppose I need to tell you that Spur is still undefeated," Cap'n Al said, putting his notebook away. "In spite of the lead Suerte held over them for a while Friday, Spur came out on top. The same old story: Slug Langenegger cleaned the bases again, only it was in the eighth inning this time, instead of the ninth."

"That's awful!" interposed Fibate. "And to think we had that bunch whipped, easy, until a couple of our men threw it out the window."

"Nine of our men!" the coach corrected Fibate tersely.

Silently, but fervently, Bronc Burnett thanked him.

"Now for some good news, purely on a hunch!" Cap'n Al said spreading a slow grin as he surveyed the sea of eager faces. "Spur plays Hope Wednesday. From the way things look to me, that fast, snappy little Hope team is just the sort to upset Spur. Hope has lost four games, true, but Greenfield only beat them two to one last week. And E. C. Barnhart, who saw the game, says they looked like a million dollars on the defense. So if Spur should lose to Hope, it means—"

"It means we've got to clean Tatum's linen!" Chic Stahl broke in impulsively. "We've just *got* to, gang! Are we ready to practice?"

Cap'n Al shook his head. "There's one thing more. Last Friday an unfortunate thing occurred. I was practically accused of showing favoritism."

Bronc and Fat went tense, though no longer did they watch the coach. Their eyes were down now.

"It was insinuated," Cap'n Al went on, his tones crisply sharp, "that I was nursing a grudge at the expense of Sonora's chance to win the game. And when—"

"That's not just it, sir!" The words cracked like blasts from an automatic. Bronc Burnett, his eyes blazing now, boring straight into Cap'n Al Carter, climbed quickly to his feet. "You've got Fat wrong! He had no idea of hinting that you were playing favorites!"

"Bronc's right, Coach!" Fat Crompton declared, also getting to his feet to stand beside his pal. "It was just— aw, you know, in the heat of a game sometimes a fellow blurts out things that keep him awake nights afterward. I'm awful sorry for what happened. And even if you suspend us from now on, we still want to help the team practice. We'll do all we can for—"

"Sit down—both of you!"

Bronc and Fat hesitated momentarily, then obeyed. They didn't lean back against the netting, however, but sat stiffly erect, their steady gaze on the coach.

"There were several reasons why I didn't send Burnett to the mound last week," he said. "Besides the fact that Pitch Carson has been a known producer for two years, maybe you noticed that Mesquite had eight left-handed batters in their line-up. Fair hitters, too. So, it seemed likely that they would pump balls by the bushel into right field. Burnett has been covering that pasture like a tent—you all know that. All right, let's see what happened!" The coach threw a quick glance over at Fibate. "How many put-outs did Bronc make in right?"

"Eight, sir!"

"You see? Eight put-outs, and he only played seven innings! Why, that's almost a record!"

"The best was Ernest Paddock of Greenfield, playing center against Vocant two years ago," Fibate contributed importantly. "He put out eleven. But Paddock was an all-round player—he could hit!"

"Anyhow," the coach resumed, "our strategy was working. Mesquite was hitting to right, and we were winning the game. Then in the seventh, when it became necessary to relieve Pitch, I did the only natural thing, a fundamental that is as old as baseball! I put in a portsider against their left-handed hitters. You saw what happened. Lefty fanned seven in his three innings. They scored a couple of times, but it wasn't Lefty's fault.

"Now, get out there. And start hustling!"

The team leaped into action, all except Bronc Burnett and Fat Crompton.

Bronc grinned at the coach. "Me, too?"

"Yes, you, too!"

"Gee! That's swell! Thank you, sir!" Bronc trotted happily to the side lines, grabbed a ball, and stood pounding it into his glove while he waited for Fat Crompton.

But it was several minutes before Fat left the coach. And instead of signaling Bronc for a throw, he came striding quickly to him. The big boy's face was unnaturally flushed.

"I stayed to explain things a little better to Cap'n Al," he said. "I told him the whole trouble had started because

I didn't think he realized just how good a pitcher you were."

"What did he say?"

"Not much," grinned Fat. "But plenty, too!"

"What do you mean?"

"He's promised to bat against you himself this afternoon. My invitation seemed to make him a little sore. Anyhow, he said he would be glad to accept the challenge whenever we were ready!"

Bronc gaped in amazement.

"The challenge?" he muttered. "Why, you dizzy yip-yap! Why, as a diplomat, you'd need help to bat zero!"

"Not at all, suh!" Fat Crompton winked. "This is your one sweet chance to establish yourself, pardner! You've got the speed and the curves to make him eat out of your hand. And after today, you'll be a fixture on the mound — Hey! Where you going?"

"I'm going right over and apologize to Cap'n Al," Bronc said stiffly.

"You're not gonna let me down now, after getting you this swell chance to win your spurs?"

"Yes, exactly! Gosh, Fat! You've gone too far this time! Get out of the way!"

"Now, listen here!" With surprising speed for a lad of his bulk, Fat Crompton hustled around in front of Bronc and blocked him.

Never had Bronc seen his friend so in earnest. After a moment of indecision, during which Fat strung out arguments that would have put a lawyer to shame, Bronc allowed himself to be convinced. "But I'm going to apologize to Cap'n Al afterward!" he declared.

"Cap'n Al will be apologizing to you!" Fat predicted confidently. "Here! Let's get started!" He took the ball from Bronc's grasp, and backed away to pitcher's distance.

Fat insisted that Bronc continue with his warmup long after Bronc, himself, was ready to go. Half a dozen more fast ones. Now a curve. That broke okay, but let's try it again! Another fast one, too. And how about the slow one you learned at the ranch! Yeah, let's sample a few "floaters." Gotta mix 'em up!

"You're ready!" Fat finally conceded, as a scorching fast ball nearly tore his hand off. "I'll go tell Cap'n Al."

"And be careful how you tell him!" Bronc growled uneasily. "I don't like the smell of this. Cap'n Al is too grand a guy for us to—"

"It's for his own good. He'll thank us afterward. He'll be a good sport."

Bronc stood watching, as Fat went over to where Cap'n Al had been helping Chic Stahl on the hook slide. Presently he saw the coach turn and glance toward him. Ashamed, Bronc lowered his eyes. He bent down, pretending to tie his shoestring.

"All right, pardner! We're ready to go!"

Slowly, gloomily, Bronc Burnett strolled out to the pitching mound, a dejected, embarrassed figure, absent-mindedly pounding the ball again and again into his glove. He kept his back turned to the plate, while Fat Crompton donned his catcher's togs.

The practice field was strangely hushed. Four or five of the boys had scattered behind Bronc to shag balls in case of hits, but the rest were grouped along the third-base foul line. They weren't talking—not even to one another—just a grim, silent row of watching boys. It was hard to tell which way their loyalty lay: to their teammate, Bronc Burnett, whom they had come to realize had a terrific fast ball and a sharp-breaking curve; or to the coach, who, presumably on account of the rabbit-ears weakness, had seemed reluctant to give him another try on the mound. These, however, were the cold facts of baseball.

In addition, there was another crosscurrent: the human side. They liked Bronc. They always had—a swell guy, from a swell family. But on the other hand, Cap'n

Al Carter had won his place with them, too. It went far beyond mere admiration for his knowledge of the game and appreciation of his help; they almost worshiped him as a man.

Now the two faced each other. Bronc, the kid pitcher, out on the mound. Alfred Carter, the former captain of a big-league team, ready at the plate.

Bronc thought Cap'n Al looked years older, standing there on the left-hand side of the rubber, with Smitty's borrowed bat on his shoulder. It was a miserable deal, all right—putting the coach on such a spot before all the boys. Hang Fat Crompton, anyhow! Fat shouldn't have put him—Bronc—on such a spot, either!

There was Fat's signal: fast one, inside.

Bronc bit his lip. By Gosh, he wouldn't throw it too fast, or too close on the inside! Still, would that be double-crossing Fat? Couldn't do that, either. He'd have to play fair with his buddy. And yet, a fast one on the inside might hit Cap'n Al. Might hurt him. Cap'n Al was nearly fifty—hadn't played actively for years. Doggone it, why had he stumbled into this mess, anyhow?

"Knock it down his throat, Cap'n Al!" Fibate Jones called shrilly from the side lines.

The rest of the team merely watched, fascinated, still not taking sides.

Behind the plate Fat Crompton pounded a big fist into his mitt. "Come on, pardner! Pitch to me, Bronc—right to me!"

Bronc started his windup slowly, then increased the tempo as his left leg came up, his right arm down and back. There—the throw—medium fast, slightly inside!

Crack!

Bronc ducked, barely in time. The ball shot past his head, zooming on a line into center field. A hit in anybody's league.

"Cut out the foolishness, Burnett!" Cap'n Al taunted

him, strangely. "Put something on this one—you're playing with the men now!"

Bronc reddened. All right—you asked for it—you're gonna get it! Hope Fat calls for another fast one. Yeah, there it is! That's using your head, Fat. Gives us a chance to cross him up—he'll be looking for a curve. All right, Mr. Coach, here's the one you asked for!

Again Bronc wound up. And this time he turned loose his "Sunday pitch"—a comet-like little pellet, streaking with all the fury of his outraged one-seventy behind it.

But again Cap'n Al pasted the ball squarely, a neat drive just over third base.

"Let's have a look at your fast ball now!" he taunted Bronc. "Those slow floaters are just like meat to a hungry dog!"

Bronc fired him a curve. It started outside, then shot across a corner in the last split second. Cap'n Al rapped it for a long fly to right field. Then he hit another fast one. And he poked a change-of-pace ball straight back at Bronc, with a zip that caused Bronc to leap straight up in the air.

"That setttles it!" Bronc conceded, sailing his glove out over the row of watching boys. "From this minute on, I'm an outfielder!"

He started for the side lines.

"Stay right where you are!" Cap'n Al motioned him back to the mound. "I need you for batting practice to the rest of the team."

Somebody tossed Bronc's glove back to him. Reluctantly he returned to the slab. He tried to keep from looking at Cap'n Al. He didn't want to face the boys, either—especially Fibate. His knees felt weak. He wanted to sit down, to bury his head in his hands, but he wouldn't. Not for the world! He'd keep his chin up. He'd have to!

Fat Crompton came trudging wearily out to stand beside him. Fat reached up, putting a huge arm around Bronc's shoulder. "Don't mind that, pardner! You're still tops in my book."

"Aw, nuts! Were you blind just now?"

"That doesn't matter. Shucks! You were pitching to a big leaguer—you're only sixteen. What do you expect for two bits, anyhow?"

"If I were any good, he'd have missed *one* of them, at least. Or knocked a foul, maybe. But, doggone it, he hit them all. And I never had more stuff in my life! No, sir, Fat! I'm just not a pitcher. Why, I'm not even good enough to carry the resin bag for a pitcher.

"But, brother, I can play the outfield!" Bronc declared suddenly, his eyes beginning to flash fire. "And I can learn to hit! That's what Dad wants, anyhow."

"It isn't what you want."

Bronc was silent for a moment. "Yes," he said, then, "maybe it is. I know it sounds a little goofy, Fat, but I'm sorta narrow-minded about this 'mediocrity' stuff. Nobody ought to be satisfied, ever, with just being run-of-the-mill caliber in anything. It doesn't matter so much whether a fellow actually makes the top. We can't all get there, of course, because there isn't room. But, doggone it, everybody ought to try—to have ambitions!

"That's the way I feel about this baseball business," Bronc went on. "I want to be a real player, if not in the box, then in the outfield. And if I can just learn to hit the way I can field and throw, maybe there's a chance to—"

"Hey!" The coach's voice jerked them back to realities. "If we don't get started, we'll need some lanterns!"

"Yes, sir!"

Fat Crompton turned and trotted to his position behind the plate. Bronc glanced at the batter. Little Peedink Harrell.

"Okay, Peedink! Right where you like 'em, fellow!"

He threw the ball about waist high, slightly outside.

Peedink Harrell caught it in the fat part of his club, propelled it solidly into right field.

Cap'n Al kept Bronc on the hill that afternoon until he was staggering, sweat streaming down into his eyes, and soaked to the waist. But instead of going to the bench, or flopping down beside the equally exhausted Crompton when relief finally did come, Bronc picked out his bat and joined the hitters awaiting their turns. Outfielders had to hit. And to hit, you gotta practice!

He didn't get a chance to hit that day, though, as Cap'n Al called a break after the boy ahead of Bronc hit his third successive drive off Pitch Carson.

"Set up the blackboard. We'll have a little skull practice now," the coach ordered Fibate Jones, when the sweating, puffing, restless boys had sprawled in their accustomed huddle before the wire netting. "Now copy off the standings!"

"I don't have to copy them, sir! I've got it all inside my head!"

Fibate wrote rapidly, then stepped aside for the team to see:

Position	Teams	Won	Lost	Percentage
1.	Spur	6	0	1.000
2.	Sonora	5	1	.833
3.	Greenfield	5	1	.833
4.	Tatum	4	2	.667
5.	Hope	2	4	.333
6.	Mesquite	2	4	.333
7.	Suerte	2	4	.333
8.	Concho	2	4	.333
9.	Vocant	2	4	.333
10.	Lakewood	0	6	.000

"These figures are pretty much self-explanatory," Cap'n Al said, walking over to the blackboard with a piece of splintered bat for a pointer. "You can see that Greenfield has just as good a position as ours. Tied for second. And they have about the same schedule ahead. Besides having to play each other in two weeks, we each have to play Tatum. And at the time we're playing Vocant on the second of May, they'll be playing Suerte; not much difference there, as Suerte and Vocant are about equal.

"However, that isn't what I wanted to talk to you about this afternoon," Cap'n Al continued seriously. "We'll do our worrying about Greenfield when the time comes. In the meantime, how about Tatum? We play there Wednesday. That's the day after tomorrow. Tatum, you can see, is right behind us. If they beat us Wednesday, they'll be up there on Greenfield's heels. They'll even be within fighting distance of the title itself, because they still have games to play with both Spur and Greenfield, the only teams above them.

"Okay. Now, with that prospect," Cap'n Al inquired, "what will be Tatum's frame of mind when they take the field against us Wednesday?"

"I can answer that one," said Peedink Harrell. "They'll be like a bulldog looking for cats!"

"That's still an understatement," the coach chuckled. "But, at least, you've got the general idea.

"Now," he continued, "let's have a look at this Tatum bunch. What do we know about them? Nothing—except the record! We know that they have beaten Hope, Vocant, Suerte, and Lakewood. We know, also, that none of these four teams was able to break loose against them; not one in the bunch scored as many as three runs. Vocant didn't score at all!

"On the other hand, two teams have beaten Tatum. Let's look at those games: Mesquite turned the trick two weeks ago, one to nothing; and last Friday, playing without its regular pitcher, Tatum dropped its game to

Concho in the tenth inning by two to one. So, what does that tell us about the team we're going to play Wednesday?"

Trail Drover's hand went up. "Tough!" he predicted. "It means they're not overly strong with the stick, maybe—but, boy, what a defense!"

"Exactly! And if we're to be held from our usual high scoring, we'll have to counter by plugging every possible leak in our defense. Of course, it may happen that we'll pound them to cover—most of you are hitting well. But on the other hand, I'm not going to overlook practice for the remainder of this afternoon on our ball handling.

"As you probably know, also," Cap'n Al continued, "Tatum is clear down in the flatlands—one hundred and seventy-five miles from here. We will leave in a school bus at one o'clock tomorrow. We are to be guests of the girls' domestic-science classes for a joint dinner with the Tatum team tomorrow night—at which time, I believe, we have been asked to contribute one stunt, as part of the evening's entertainment. Is that still the plan, Fibate?"

"Yes, sir! And I'm cooking up a dandy!"

"Good! Now, everybody out on the field—everybody, that is, except Burnett and Crompton. I'll have a few words with them in private."

The team raced onto the field.

Bronc grinned dryly at his coach. "Shall I turn around, and bend over? I've got a good kick coming to me!"

Cap'n Al shook his head. Strangely, he was smiling—a friendly smile, too!

"Burnett," he said, "I never make up my mind, for sure, until just before a game starts. But from the way things look now, I'm going to send you to the hill against Tatum."

"Aw, no, sir! Not me! I just 'took the cure,' out there

a while ago. I haven't any more business trying to pitch than a hog has with a bicycle!"

The coach laid a hand on Bronc's arm. He was still smiling. "I don't want to give you a swelled head," he confided, "but this much I will say: You lack training, of course, but as far as your arm itself is concerned, you've got as much natural stuff as I ever saw on a kid. And I've looked at plenty! Now, does that make you feel better?"

"It would, sure—if I hadn't just seen you bust my 'Sunday pitches' all over the lot!"

"Oh, that—" Cap'n Al Carter grinned boyishly. "I was able to hit you, yes, but only because I knew, *ahead*, just what you were going to throw me."

"You knew that?" Fat Crompton gasped amazedly. "Why, doggone it, I kept my signals covered! And I never once gave out any chatter I'd ever used before. I don't see how—"

"Bronc told me himself!" Cap'n Al chuckled. "That's something, by the way, we'll have to work on before he takes the slab Wednesday. Every time he gets ready to throw a fast one, he clamps his lips together and hitches at his belt, as if to make sure his uniform doesn't bind him at the waist. And when he gets ready for a curve, he always digs in the dirt—unconsciously, of course—with the toe of his right foot. And for his change of pace, he always moistens the fingers of his right hand. So, you see. . . ."

"Holy smokes!" Bronc muttered. "You really put a fellow under the microscope, don't you?"

"I'll put you under a steam roller, if you don't win for us on Wednesday!" Cap'n Al said grimly, again becoming the serious-eyed coach of a baseball team. "Now, get in to the shower room—and take care of that arm. The rest of us will stay and practice on giving you support. Go on. What're you waiting for?"

Bronc hadn't moved, except to rub one shaking hand

across his chin. "I'm afraid to move," he said. "Afraid it'll wake me up—and how I'm loving this dream!"

"It won't be a dream when they start working on those rabbit ears of yours. It'll be a nightmare!"

"Rabbit ears? Aw, that's ancient history, Coach. I'll show you on Wednesday!"

Cap'n Al studied the husky youth intently. "I wish the rest of us could be as sure of that," he said, turning thoughtfully to the practice.

Chapter 10

A NIGHT TO REMEMBER

THE ride down into the flatlands was uneventful, save for the heat and the dust. Accustomed as the Sonora boys were to the piny fragrance of the cooler mountains, they were a fairly quiet group when they finally reached Tatum about six-thirty. But refreshing baths quickly worked a change.

What the heck—they hadn't come here for the joy ride, anyhow! This was a business trip; the business of lifting Tatum's baseball scalp, and going on up the wobbly, rickety ladder to a championship.

After Tatum would come Vocant, two days later the same week, with Greenfield the following Friday. Then if Cap'n Al's hunch proved correct, and Hope did bump Spur for a loss, they would finish the season in a tie. That's what they wanted; another crack at high-flying Spur. This time they would show Slug Langenegger and his crowd!

As for Vocant and Greenfield . . . Well, Greenfield would be tough, of course, but Vocant was a push-over. Ninth placers, barely above Lakewood. A good team for five or six innings, maybe, but their lone pitcher was a slim kid of seventeen, who simply couldn't stand the gaff over the full route. They'd cop that one, easy enough. Then the more formidable Greenfield team would put them in just the trim they would need to whip Spur.

But first, Cap'n Al kept reminding them, they had to get over the hump with Tatum.

Well, they would. Shucks! Tatum was just another bunch of boys—not supermen, at all—just plain, ordinary human beings! Wasn't it John McGraw who scoffed about tough opponents: "They put their pants on one leg at a time just as we do, don't they?"

Oh, they'd have to play ball, of course, They expected to! But there was no use in a team's being blind to its own abilities. They had the hitting: a team average of .314, twenty points better than Spur, according to Fibate Jones. And Fibate didn't miss when it came to figures. They had good fielding, too; an .897 average, which was plenty good for high school ball.

They'd beat Tatum, all right. Heck—that's what they'd ridden a hundred and seventy-five hot, dusty miles for!

The dinner that night turned out to be a full-fledged banquet. One of the large first-floor rooms at the schoolhouse had been decorated with the school colors, blue and white, and the tables were arranged in the shape of a huge horseshoe. The open end of the horseshoe was toward the kitchen, for convenience in serving, and at the opposite end a large American flag hung from the wall, some ten feet behind the chair reserved for the Superintendent of Schools.

Cap'n Al Carter sat on the right of Superintendent Roger Q. Lacey, while the Tatum coach sat on his left. The other chairs along that end were occupied by the two team captains. And flanking them were the two student team managers, who were to have charge of the program afterward.

Around the outer rim of the shoe sat the teams, alternating: a Tatum player, then one from Sonora, and so on. Bronc Burnett had taken a seat near one end, between two of Tatum's substitute outfielders. Fat Crompton was about midway of the opposite side.

It was an excellent meal, once the players broke the formality of the domestic-science girls, who had made the error of serving hard-to-manage fried chicken. So by the time they had reached the ice-cream-and-cake stage, the room was a happy, noisy place.

"We've got a real stunt cooked up on Mr. Lacey," one of the Tatum players confided to Bronc. "He's a good sport, and—"

"Sh-h-h-h!"

The Superintendent of Schools had risen from his seat.

He was a man of medium height, with coal-black hair, parted exactly in the middle, and with a neatly groomed black mustache. He seemed a trifle overdressed for the occasion, in his white linen suit with a large red rose in the lapel, but there was no denying the friendliness of his smile or the ready applause with which his students greeted him.

"Mr. Carter, Coach Ledbetter, members of the Sonora and Tatum high school baseball teams," he began formally. "It is always a source of extreme pleasure for us to come together on this annual occasion, at which time, each year, we sit down in mingled fellowship and gaiety with the conference team of our choice.

"I want to assure you, good people of Sonora, that this year's selection was not in the least difficult. For your splendid record, not only on the field of conflict, but also in recognition of your clean sportsmanship, we consider ourselves honored by your presence.

"Tomorrow we expect a glorious game. May the best team win! But, also—" he winked, "may the best team be Tatum!"

"Yeah, Prof!"

"Atta boy, Prof!"

The Sonora delegation merely exchanged wry grins.

"At any rate," Superintendent Lacey continued, "no matter who wins on the morrow, tonight I want to assure you of your welcome to Tatum. And please remember that we shall be looking forward to having you back here with us again."

The room shook with applause, as the Superintendent sat down. Cap'n Al Carter was on his feet immediately. He waited until the room had quieted, then glanced down at his host.

"I'm not much of a hand at making speeches," he said, "but when it comes to reading people, I don't take a back seat to anybody. And if I were given the job of rounding up and sorting all the people in the Sapello Valley, there would be a special corral set aside for you Tatum folks. And it would carry the label, 'Thoroughbreds.'

"As for the game tomorrow, all I can say is: we're going to play hard all the way. And I sincerely hope you end up as the second-best team in our whole conference!"

A chuckle swept the room, as the significance of Cap'n Al's remark dawned on them.

"Anyhow, thanks a lot for this fine food tonight," he concluded, "and for the swell way you've treated us all!"

He sat down. Again the group applauded enthusiastically.

"The next portion of our program," Superintendent Lacey announced, "will be the stunts: one, I understand, from each team. For some reason, certainly unknown to me, Tatum is to take the impolite position of first. Are you ready, boys?"

Two grinning youngsters, one carrying an accordion with its strap looped around his neck, and the other with a violin, stepped into the center of the horseshoe.

"Our special number tonight," the accordionist explained, "is to be a take-off on the famed baseball epic, 'Casey at the Bat,' with full apologies to the original author, Ernest Lawrence Thayer. So, with your permission, gentlemen, we proudly present: 'Lacey at the Bat'!"

Two dozen pair of eyes shifted to Superintendent Roger Q. Lacey. They saw him begin to redden, but he forced a grin, nevertheless, motioning for the show to go on.

The musicans started playing with a flourish, then softened. The accordionist, in perfect time, recited:

"It looked extremely rocky for the Tatum nine
    that day;
    The score stood two to four, with but an
      inning left to play.
So when Bowen died at second, an' Dub Andrus
    did the same,
    A pallor wreathed the features of the patrons of
      the game."

A chorus of snickers interrupted the narrator. The horseshoe of laughing boys stopped the show temporarily, gradually quieting to let it go on for perhaps another minute.

"Then from the gladdened multitude went up a
    joyous yell,
    It rumbled in the mountaintops, it rattled in
      the dell;
It struck upon the hillside and rebounded on the
    flat;
    For *Lacey*, mighty *Lacey*, was advancing to the
      bat."

Suddenly a baseball player, completely uniformed even to his spikes, entered the room. Clackety-clack—clackety-clack—clack—clack— He paused in the center of the horseshoe. A delighted howl rose from the boys as they noted, more closely, the way he was dressed. Not only the uniform of Tatum High School, but from beneath his up-tilted cap they could see his black hair was parted exactly in the middle. He even sported a black mustache like that of Superintendent Lacey. The bat on his shoulder was ludicrously large; bigger, even, than a fence post.

When the laughter and buzz of comment subsided once more, the "ballplayer" began to pantomime the words and story resumed by the musicians:

> "There was ease in Lacey's manner as he stepped
> into his place,
> There was pride in Lacey's bearing and a smile
> on Lacey's face.
> And when responding to the cheers he lightly
> doffed his hat,
> No stranger in the crowd could doubt 'twas
> Lacey at the bat."

Again the narrator had to pause, as amused snickers swelled into a roar. At the head of the table, Superintendent Roger Q. Lacey had lowered his head, shielding his face with one hand. The room quieted. Once more "the mighty Lacey" began to pantomime, while the narrator hurried on to the famous last verse:

> "Oh, somewhere in this favored land the sun is
> shining bright,
> The band is playing somewhere, and somewhere
> hearts are light;
> And somewhere men are laughing, and somewhere
> children shout,
> But there is no joy in Tatum: Mighty Lacey
> has struck out!"

As "the mighty Lacey" completed his ferocious swing and clattered from the room, boys shouted and hooted

131

and patted one another on the back in delirious pandemonium. Superintendent Roger Q. Lacey, his face and neck fully as red as the flower he wore in his lapel, signaled again and again for silence; but each time a new outbreak would send the room into bedlam for several more minutes.

"Boys," he said finally, when he was able to make himself heard, "I am practically forced to congratulate you. You have succeeded in doing something where Nature herself has failed. You have made me a ballplayer!"

Again bedlam broke loose, stamping of feet, whistling and clapping.

"He's a good sport, all right," Bronc Burnett whispered, leaning over behind the Tatum player on his right toward Chic Stahl.

"Sure. He's okay."

"Our next specialty," Superintendent Lacey announced, "is the feature by our guests of the evening. From the paper that has just been handed me, I notice that it will be a radio show—a play-by-play account, in advance, of the game tomorrow. Well, well! How revealing this should be! Gentlemen, I present young Mr. Reginald Jones, alias 'Fibate,' and Harvey Dillon, alias 'Wasp'!"

Fibate and Wasp rose, made a quick bow in response to the applause that promptly greeted them, and then took their places near the head of the table. Wasp was carrying a microphone now, which he set up in view of all; and meanwhile Bill Burnham had quietly risen from his seat to push a large, previously arranged radio cabinet out into the center of the horseshoe.

While these preparations were being made, Chic Stahl pulled his chair over close to Bronc. "You mentioned something about their prof being a good sport a while ago. Well, I've always thought you were a good sport, too. But I wonder how good?"

"What do you mean?"

"I was just thinking—how would you like to help Fibate with his stunt tonight?"

Bronc grinned. "The only way I'll help Fibate," he said, "is give a pull on the rope if he ever wants to hang himself!"

"Aw, it isn't that bad, and you know it. But I'm really serious. After all, this isn't just for Fibate—it's for Sonora —for all of us. We want to give Tatum a show they'll never forget. We'd thought some about asking Fat Crompton to help with a certain part, but he's got some rather stiff-necked ideas about loyalty to his friends, and we were afraid he might explode the whole thing. Anyhow, I agreed to take the part instead. But it's just occurred to me, if you'd be a good enough sport to—"

"Sorta twisting a fellow's arm, aren't you, hinting about his sportsmanship?"

"It's for Sonora. Would that make any difference?"

Bronc frowned. "What is it you want?"

Chic cupped both hands to Bronc's ear. He whispered rapidly for perhaps a minute, then leaned back. "Are you game?"

"I think it smells! But I'll agree. They'll remember this night in Tatum long after they're forgotten the Fourth of July and Christmas. Maybe— Well, okay then! Slip me the old blunderbuss. I'll go through with it. But durn your hide, if—"

"Sh-h-h-h! They're ready!"

Wasp Dillon had tested the public-address system, and taking a sheet of yellow paper from his pocket he stepped to the microphone.

"Ladies and gentlemen of the radio audience," he began, the words booming distinctly out of the radio amplifier, which Bill Burnham had pushed into the center of the room. "We are going to switch you to the Tatum baseball park, where Fibate Jones is waiting to give you a play-by-play account of the game now in progress between Tatum and Sonora High Schools. All right. Come in, Fibate!"

A momentary pause. The audience grinned expectantly, all eyes on the radio rather than the microphone and speakers.

"Good afternoon, everybody! This is Fibate Jones, bringing you the sterling story of one of the most unusual games ever staged on anybody's diamond. We're speaking from the press box, directly behind home plate, looking out above a seething mass of screaming maniacs, who have gone completely mad over the fantastic spectacle that has been unfolding for some three innings now —three innings, ladies and gentlemen, of the most super-colossal baseball extravaganza of all time.

"The score—after only three innings, mind you—is: Tatum thirty-six; Sonora thirty-six. Get that? Tied up at thirty-six all, in the last of the third! Rabbit Ears Burnett is pitching for Sonora. Rabbit Ears, you may remember, is the lad with the strong back and the weak mind, who—"

"Hold on there, Fibate!" Bronc Burnett started to his feet, shaking his fist at his tormentor. "Stop that—"

"Aw, sit down, Bronc!" Chic Stahl caught hold of Bronc and pulled him back into his chair. "It's all in fun!"

"But he's carrying it too far! There's no use in his getting so personal!" Bronc growled.

"As I was saying, ladies and gentlemen of the radio audience," Fibate's voice resumed through the loud speaker, "this has been an amazing spectacle out here this afternoon. Sonora is in the field now—there's nobody down—the bases are loaded. A hit will break the tie.

"Rabbit Ears Burnett has the ball. He's standing out on the mound looking at the Tatum batsman. Now he rubs the ball on his pants—he's getting ready— There's the stretch! There's the— No, wait a minute, folks! Once more this supersensitive would-be pitcher picks up a familiar sound from the crowd. Let's see what it is this time. Oh, yes! Somebody in white— Some girl in a white hat over there along the first-base line has called something to Rabbit Ears. He stops, and— There! He throws her a kiss! Can you imagine that, ladies and gentlemen? With the bases full, and—"

"You'd better lay off of me, Fibate!" Bronc yelled.

"Aw, let him go!"

"Sure, go ahead, Fibate! It's all in fun!"

"And now Cap'n Al Carter, the Sonora coach, starts out to the mound. He stops at the base line. He calls something to Rabbit Ears. Rabbit Ears nods, then waves him back. Now, here comes Cap'n Al back to the bench. Rabbit Ears is ready again to pitch. Now, if only somebody else doesn't say something that those supersensitive ears will pick up—I believe he's going to pitch this time. I believe— No, I'm sorry, ladies and gentlemen! Again somebody in the stands has made a remark that Rabbit Ears feels called on to answer. Again the game is being delayed. Rabbit Ears has left the mound. He's walking this way—down here toward home plate. Let's see if we can pick up what he is yelling at the fan who—"

Bronc jumped to his feet.

"I'll help you pick it up, you barb-tongued little coyote!" he roared, shaking his fist savagely at Fibate. "One more word out of you, and I'll—"

"Aw, sit down, Bronc!"

"I won't sit down!"

"But it's all in fun, and—"

Chic Stahl attempted to pull Bronc back, but Bronc knocked his hand roughly aside. He climbed up onto his chair. Again he shook his fist at Fibate. Chic succeeded in grabbing Bronc's trouser leg momentarily, but Bronc kicked out at him viciously, shoving him back.

The room was in near-bedlam now, with all of the boys taking sides, everybody trying to talk at once.

Suddenly Bronc whipped a pistol from under his coat.

135

It was a huge thing—a double-action forty-five. Still standing on the chair, towering above them all, he brandished the gun. "You've had this coming to you all season, Fibate!" he yelled. "Now take it!"

Fibate screamed. Two roaring, deafening blasts spurted from the gun barrel. Simultaneously Chic Stahl leaped for the electric-light switch. The room went dark as the yelling, stampeding boys scrambled wildly for places of cover.

Then the room quieted, save for tense, muffled breathing.

Bronc felt his way through the darkness to the wall switch, touched Chic on the arm. "Whew! How it worked!" he chuckled delightedly. "Didn't those blank cartridges make a racket?"

"I'll say! You're a real actor, Bronc, and a real sport! It took a man to—"

A shrill scream, unmistakably the voice of Fibate Jones, knifed the stillness.

"Oh! Ouch! Somebody—help!"

"Better turn on the lights," Bronc advised.

Chic flipped the switch. Instant, dazzling light again flooded the banquet room.

For a moment the room looked absolutely deserted, save for Fibate Jones and Wasp Dillon, who were still back of the speaker's microphone. Wasp Dillon stood erect and was holding his sides, while Fibate was doubled over with laughter.

Gradually, here and there, heads began to appear from beneath the table. Eyes bulged at first, then as the boys saw that the whole thing had been a hoax they grinned sheepishly. Superintendent Lacey joined the merriment, even though his freshly starched white linen suit was now a soiled mess.

However, the party was definitely "off." Less than half of the original crowd was left in the room. Two opened windows explained how and where the rest had gone. And the odds were a million to nothing that not a single one of the fugitives would show himself again that night.

By twos and threes the Sonora team came straggling back to the hotel, and by nine-thirty they were all in their rooms. Bronc found Fat Crompton sitting on the edge of the bed, his face in his hands.

"Bad news?" Bronc inquired, knowing his roommate.

"The worst kind."

"How come?"

"You're not pitching tomorrow," Fat said slowly, without glancing up. "Cap'n Al was just in. I'm to catch, all right. Drake Yoder turned an ankle when he jumped out of the window. But it's *you* we'll be needing in that battery tomorrow."

"Gosh! I hate that, Fat. Was Cap'n Al sore?"

"No. That's another thing that baffles me. He was nice as pie. Just said he'd see us in the morning."

Why did Cap'n Al change his mind about starting me? wondered Bronc. Hope I'll get a chance to find out tomorrow.

ON THE CLIMB

SOMEHOW, it just didn't work out for Bronc Burnett and Cap'n Al to get together before game time the next day. Not that they were deliberately avoiding each other —at least, not in Bronc's case—their trails just didn't seem to cross in the routine of late breakfast, a short visit to the new agriculture department of Tatum High School, light lunch, and one-hour period of rest in their rooms before going out to the park.

They paired off for several minutes, getting limbered up. Sweat came easily. Too easily! It was going to be much hotter, down here in this irrigated flatland.

"I just can't seem to work up any pep," Bill Burnham complained.

"You will!" Cap'n Al told him. "You'll be livelier than a grasshopper on a hot stove this afternoon, or I'll put a firecracker under your tail. Now, let's get our hitting practice. Red," indicating Red Bailey. "You're the first chucker. Peedink, grab your bat. Dump one, then hit three. Everybody hustle!"

They had time for each player to get two turns at the plate, then resumed a pepper game along the side lines.

Bronc was throwing to Fat Crompton when the coach finally accosted him for the first time.

"You're on the bench today, Burnett. I'm using Pitch Carson."

138

"Yes, sir."

"Crompton, you go over and receive for Pitch. Start him in easy—George Fitzpatrick will keep him going while you join our infield workout later. Then you can taper him off just before play starts."

"Yes, sir!" Fat trotted away.

Cap'n Al started to leave, hesitated momentarily, then turned again to Bronc. "I'm sorry, Burnett. But after that affair last night—well, you haven't got any business whatever on the mound."

"Gee, coach, why not?"

"It's not that I object to the stunt—as a matter of fact, I thought it was rich—even if I did crawl under the table myself! But by now, the whole community will know about it. They'll all be curious to see the famous Rabbit Ears, and they would hoot and jeer and mock you clear out of town."

Bronc stared in amazement. He hadn't thought of that.

"I'll want you to keep warm, however," the coach added. "There's no telling what may happen today. We must not let last evening's good fellowship with these boys throw us off guard. Tatum is still determined to win this game. I might send you to the hill any time, so be ready."

"Yes, sir!"

The game started loosely. Both teams, young and playing under strain, committed errors in the early innings. By the fifth, Tatum held a four-to-one lead. Sonora had been hitting the ball, but three fast little hawks in the opposing Tatum outfield had come through, time and again, with spectacular running catches to nip each threat of the visitors.

With two down in the fifth, however, "Slow Molasses" Smith caught hold of one for a clean single over short. Bill Burnham, next up, stalled for a three-two pitch and then propelled it out of the park for a clean home run. Four to three!

But there it stayed. Still four to three as the last of the eighth rolled around. And with the eighth came trouble for Pitch Carson.

"You go down and start throwing—fast!" Cap'n Al ordered Bronc, as Pitch gave up a base on balls, following a Tatum two-bagger.

The Tatum pitcher came to bat. He was a short, stocky youth, who pitched right-handed but batted left. Fat Crompton, the back of his uniform grimy and wet with sweat, waddled out to reassure Pitch Carson and give him a breather. Fat had caught a good game. An *honest* game, considering the fact that he might secretly have hoped for Pitch to fail so Bronc would be called to the mound.

Now he and Pitch chatted for a moment, then Fat slapped him on the back and returned to position.

"Let's go, gang! Everybody alive! Make him hit to me, Pitch. . . ."

Ball one. Ball two. On a weak batter—

Cap'n Al got up from the bench. But just as he started to motion for Bronc, Pitch grooved a strike. A long foul went for strike two. The coach sat down.

Meanwhile, along the third-base line, his back to the ball game, Bronc Burnett was throwing rapidly to George Fitzpatrick.

The Tatum pitcher grounded out to Smith at first, but both runners advanced. Men on second and third now, with only one down. Dub Andrus, the Tatum lead-off man, came to bat. He was a smiling, relaxed, black-haired boy, with two hits and a walk already to his credit that day. The crowd gave him a tremendous hand. He'd pound them in a run, all right. Maybe two!

"Time out!"

Cap'n Al waved his pitcher to the bench. He started out to meet Bronc Burnett, who, like all well-coached bull-pen pitchers, had delayed long enough to get in a few additional throws to his catcher. Now Bronc turned, coming in toward the coach.

"Feel all right, lad?"

A physician's stethoscope would have said, "No!" Heart pounding too rapidly. Nerves taut. Breathing too fast. But Bronc Burnett, now that the big moment had come, forced his most casual grin.

"Fine, sir!"

The coach linked arms with him. Together they entered the diamond, walking over to the mound where Fat Crompton and Trail Drover stood waiting for them.

"Good boy, Bronc!" said Trail. "We're all behind you!"

Fat merely grinned his welcome.

"Now, here's the situation," Cap'n Al said to Bronc. "Runners on second and third. One down. Get that? Only one down, and runners on second and third. Their lead-off man is up. He's got a good eye, and he's fast. So I want him passed. Take no chances—just four straight, outside balls, filling the bases. Then maybe we can pull a double play, or maybe you can handle the next batter yourself. Do you understand, too, Crompton?"

"Yes, sir!"

"Good! Now, one thing more: After you've passed Andrus, filling the bases, watch out for a bunt. That would be sound baseball. Eighth inning—a one-run lead —a fast, tricky little batter like Bowen at the plate. Watch it, lads!"

"I'll bet you could tell if they gave the signal," Drover ventured.

"I could—yes. I've already picked out all of their signals. But I'm leaving it up to you boys. And I scarcely need to add, Burnett: the fate of our whole season is pretty much in your hands right now. So, watch those rabbit ears. Good luck!"

Cap'n Al turned and walked to the bench. Fat Crompton pressed the ball into Bronc's hand, grinned out through his mask, started to speak but couldn't. He went back to position, laid his mask on the ground beside him, and took Bronc's five warmup throws. Then as the batter stepped to the plate, ready to resume play, Fat Crompton moved several feet to the right of his usual position. Without putting on his mask, he signaled Bronc to begin. The crowd caught on instantly.

Two big events: an "intentional pass," and Rabbit Ears himself on the mound!

The crowd responded with a concerted roar that rattled the park, but it seemed miles away to Bronc. "—*the fate of our whole season . . . in your hands . . .*" still dinned in his ears, drowning everything else. The four deliberate "balls" he threw to Fat helped to steady him. So when the umpire announced, "Take your base!" Bronc was grimly ready.

The bases full now. Only one down. Bowen, another dark-haired, shifty little batter, approached the plate for Tatum. He was going to hit right-handed.

Before signaling a pitch, however, Fat Crompton came hurrying out to Bronc. "Coach has left it up to us," he said. "I've just been thinking, if this guy wants to bunt, let's make it easy for him."

"You mean, try for a force at home?"

"Sure—deliberately!"

Bronc looked his buddy straight in the eye. "I know what that will mean," he said slowly. "You must have a lot of confidence in me."

"Sure! Want to risk it?"

"Okay!"

Fat trotted back to the plate. Bronc pulled out his handkerchief, mopped sweat from his forehead, pocketed the handkerchief, and pulled his cap down tight. Behind him the team went into its jargon:

"What do you say in there, Bronc? Make him hit to

142

me! Bases full, gang—tag any base—play for the easy one, then get two! Let's get a double. . . ."

Meanwhile, the crowd was on its feet, calling for a hit, shouting advice, hooting at the calm boy with the slim waist and the wide shoulders, who now stood alone in the center of the diamond. Tatum one run ahead, but with the bases full, a ball game would still ride on every pitch.

Bronc took Fat's signal—a low, fast one, outside. Good stuff! If the gent bunts this one, it will be almost sure to roll down the first-base line. Well, I'll be ready! He studied the batter. The little fellow seemed to be putting up a mighty savage front for one of his size; well back in the box, feet together, and brandishing his bat with all the menace of a two-hundred-pound six-footer. Too obvious, Bronc thought. A dead give-away. Trying to bluff us into playing deep.

"We'll have a bear trap set for you, sonny!" he muttered.

Bronc took his stance on the mound where he could watch the runners. Legs spraddled, his body squarely facing third base, he clutched the ball with both hands against the lower part of his chest. The runner on third tantalized him by creeping farther from the bag—six feet —eight feet—ten feet— Bronc shifted his weight slightly, getting ready to try for him. The runner seemed to notice. He eased back toward third. It was the moment Bronc had waited for.

Instantly, without a windup, he delivered the ball to the plate. And as he turned it loose, he broke into a run, forward and to his left. But the batter made no attempt to bunt or to swing. The crowd hooted delightedly as Bronc turned and slowly walked back to the mound. He didn't care. They'd be singing a different tune if the batter *had* tried to bunt. In that case, he would have been in position to field the ball. And the runner on third

143

would not have had a cinch, either—Bronc had kept him so close to the bag that he probably couldn't have made home. Yeah, let 'em holler!

The fact that it was "Ball one" on the batter didn't matter. Bronc still had a margin. The batter would probably go for this next one. Usually these plays were set for the second pitched ball, anyhow, rather than the first.

What was Fat signaling? Another low one, this time over an inside corner.

In that case, Bronc figured he'd better not veer off toward the first-base line after his pitch. Might get crossed up, if the bunt went toward third instead. Better go straight down off of the mound, ready to dart either way.

"Hey, Bronc!" he heard Smith yell from first, above the noise of the crowd. "Don't forget these other runners. They're both taking mighty big leads on you."

Bronc nodded. "I know—but it's the man on third I've got to keep the hobbles on!"

"You might pick one of these other gents off."

"I'll keep it in mind."

Bronc stepped to the slab, again taking his spraddle-legged position facing third. The runner crept cautiously along the base line. Now he paused, not daring to venture farther, and yet ready to slide back to safety if Bronc made a throw for him.

On beyond the runner, Bronc saw that Lefty Lear had begun to warm up for Sonora. Cap'n Al wasn't taking any chances!

"Don't forget this man over here!" Smith called again. "He's taking more liberties than a traveling salesman with—"

Suddenly, quickly, Bronc whipped his pitch to the plate. But even in that split second, the canny little batter had changed his stance. Squarely facing Bronc now, both hands spread apart on the bat in front of him, he was ready.

A bunt, all right! Which way? There—toward third! Bronc, already dashing forward, swerved to the right and kept going. The man on third was running in, too.

Bronc scooped up the ball, started to toss to Fat Crompton, who had his mask off and was straddling the plate. Then he noted the speeding runner almost on top of him. He tagged the runner himself.

"Quick, Bronc! To first!"

Bronc whirled. He shot the ball with a savagery that nearly lifted their first baseman into the air, but Smith held it. The runner was out by a step.

Double play! Three down!

Heavy hands pounded Bronc on the back, as he trouped to the bench, where other teammates, jabbering excitedly, were waiting to congratulate him. He dropped on the bench beside Pitch Carson. Pitch laid a hand on his knee.

"That's chucking, Bronc, boy!"

"Shucks!" growled Fibate, from behind. "He only threw two balls at the plate."

"That's all it took!" Pitch Carson defended. "That, and some mighty quick thinking. It was the heat that got me," he went on to explain. "That last inning it seemed as if I couldn't throw hard enough to bust an egg."

The Sonora team was excitedly sorting bats.

"You're up first, Bill! Come on, boy! Get on base. Somebody will knock you in, Bill! First of the ninth— our last bat, gang. . . ."

Bill Burnham, slugging center fielder for Sonora, pulled his cap tight on his forehead, tucked in his shirt, and walked over to the plate. He waited nonchalantly while the Tatum pitcher completed his practice throws, then stepped into the box.

The Tatum infielders were a lively, hustling group,

too: "What do you say in there, kid? Everything in your favor, little fellow! Send him back to the bench, kid. . . ."

Bill Burnham fouled the first pitch far down the first-base line. He watched two outside curves dart past. Two balls, one strike.

He hit the next one for two bases. To a man, the Sonora team was off the bench, howling like maniacs, and slapping one another on the back.

A runner on second! Nobody down! Come on, Red—knock him in, Red!

But Cap'n Al had other ideas. Instead of having Red Bailey try for a hit, he held up his closed right fist. The signal to bunt! And Red came through. On the first pitch he dumped a neat one between the pitcher and first. They threw him out easily, but Bill Burnham had advanced from second to third on the sacrifice.

The Tatum infield grouped around their pitcher, jabbering encouragement: "That's one down, kid! Never mind that! Only two more, and we go home. . . ."

Fat Crompton, dripping with sweat and puffing like a hippopotamus, slid over beside Cap'n Al. "Do you mind if I ask a question, sir?"

"What's on your mind?"

"Now, don't get me wrong," Fat began uneasily. "I'm not criticizing—just trying to learn the game. Why did you waste an 'out' on Red Bailey? A hit would have brought Bill in from second the same as from third, and we'd have had three batters to try for it, instead of only two."

"Good question," grunted Cap'n Al. "But you almost answered it yourself when you mentioned a 'hit'—that's what it would take to score a man from second. But this way, besides a hit, we've got several other chances to shove him across: A long fly to the outfield would do it; a squeeze bunt, an infield put-out, an error; a passed ball

146

on the part of the catcher; maybe even a dropped third strike that would require a hasty throw to first. See?"

Fat nodded assent admiringly, and turned again to the diamond, where play was about to be resumed.

The fateful ninth! One down. Bill Burnham waiting hopefully on third. Buck Losey at the plate.

Buck popped a high foul, which Tatum's hustling catcher bagged over near the stands. He slammed his bat down disgustedly. Two outs! How they applauded now —except from the Sonora bench!

Trail Drover went to bat. Trail was crafty, and he managed to work the Tatum pitcher for a free ticket to first. Now it was Sonora's turn to yell, while the home crowd seethed uneasily. Two down—runners camped on first and third. Fat Crompton was up. Bronc Burnett waiting on deck.

Little time was spent on Crompton. In trying to slip him a fast ball, inside, the Tatum pitcher plunked him in the ribs. Fat hobbled off to first, clutching his side.

Bronc Burnett's heart was almost in his mouth as he stepped to the plate. Two down—the last inning—bases full!

"Gee! If Dad could just be here and see this! This is one time I'm going to hit! And hit hard! I've had a lot of 'black marks' against me this year. But I'm gonna rub 'em all off today! Wonder what—"

There was a sudden commotion on the Sonora bench. Cap'n Al Carter came running over.

"Time out!" he requested the umpire. Then, turning to Bronc, he laid a hand on the husky shoulder. "I'm sorry, lad. We've got to play percentages, though. I'm sending Drake Yoder in to hit for you."

"You're taking me out of the game?"

"Yes, lad. You've only been hitting one-seventy-three, while Drake is crowding four hundred. Go on to the bench."

"Yes, sir."

Bronc walked slowly over to the Sonora side and sat down. He heard Fibate snicker behind him, but paid no attention. Fibate didn't count now. Nothing did—nothing but winning this game. Bronc put both hands to his mouth, shouting to the big lad who had succeeded him:

"Come on, Drake! Give the old pill a ride! We're all pulling for you, boy!"

Drake Yoder limped into the batter's box. His left ankle showed a bulging bandage from his leap out of the schoolhouse the night before, but otherwise he looked very much like a hitter—big shoulders, good stance—and if he had any inner qualms about being able to come through in the pinch, it did not show in his manner.

The crowd hushed as Tatum's pitcher prepared to throw. Drake, who had been swinging his bat slowly, now poised.

Ball one. Then, ball two!

"Both low and outside!" Cap'n Al muttered. "They figure, on account of his bum ankle, he won't be able to reach for one. Well, I hope they keep trying. It's just where he likes them best."

The Tatum pitcher threw again. This time Drake swung. Sure enough, it had been over an outside corner, only about knee-high. How he did smash it! The ball rocketed on a line straight for the foul flag in right field, kicked up white lime as it bounced, and then got beyond the fielder who had tried to intercept it.

Burnham crossed the plate. The score was tied! Trail Drover scored. One ahead! And here came Fat Crompton—eyes big as apples, mouth wide open, arms flailing—but he made it. Sonora now led, six to four!

Meanwhile, seeing the three runs safely across the plate, Red Bailey held the injured Drake Yoder up at first, and Cap'n Al promptly sent George Fitzpatrick in to run for him. The crowd sat in stunned silence as

148

Drake limped back to the Sonora bench. But there his teammates gave him a hero's reception, until Cap'n Al reminded them that the ball game was still in progress.

Peedink Harrell popped out to shortstop to end the inning, and Sonora sprinted onto the field. Last of the ninth. Two runs, now, to the good. They'd have to hold 'em to win! They passed the ball around with new-found pep and confidence, while Lefty Lear took his five warmup throws from the hill.

Tatum threatened immediately, as the first batter pumped a single over second base. The crowd began to yell again with new hope. But the next man drove a sharp grounder to Trail Drover on short, and Trail promptly started a twin killing that was a beauty; short to second to first. Two down. The sacks clean. Again the infield peppered the ball around.

"That's the way to go, gang! Everybody behind you, Lefty! Make him hit to me, boy! Make him hit to me. . . ."

Tatum sent in a pinch hitter. He was a tall boy with long arms, and he plainly meant business. He smashed Lefty's first pitch to left field—hard. Luck was with Sonora. A few feet either way would have netted at least a three-bagger, but the ball zoomed straight into the hands of Peedink Harrell, and the game was over.

While Wasp Dillon gathered up their equipment, the jubilant team piled into the bus. There, they quieted. Those cushions felt mighty good. Though nothing could have wiped the grins from their sweaty, dirty faces, a dozen pairs of tired eyes were closed as they drove to the hotel.

"While we're taking baths," Cap'n Al told Fibate, "there are a couple of phone calls I want you to make."

"Yes, sir?"

"First, call home. Tell 'em about the game. Then call

Spur. Find out what happened in their game with Hope."

"Yes, sir!" Fibate was off at a trot.

He was back by the time the team had finished dressing.

"I got Sonora," he announced. "Talked to the mayor, George Headrick, himself. And was he tickled!"

"How about Spur?" several voices asked simultaneously.

"Oh, that— They're tied, six to six, in the seventh inning."

Cap'n Al whistled softly between his teeth. "Another setup for Slug Langenegger, it looks like. But we'll keep our fingers crossed. Which do you want to do, boys: eat here, or drive an hour or so toward home?"

"Let's not do anything!" Fat Crompton groaned. "I don't ever want to move again, the rest of my life!" He looked it, too, but there was no sympathy coming from his exhausted teammates.

They voted to start for home immediately.

At Concho, sixty-five miles up the homeward trail to the mountains, they stopped for supper; and while the meal was being prepared, Fibate again hurried to a telephone and called Spur. He was grinning when he came back.

"Still six to six!"

"You don't say! What inning?"

"Believe it or not, the twelfth!"

A howl of delight went up from the boys. Say, little Hope might turn the trick, after all! And if they did, who would be tied for first? Right, mister! Sonora! Yeah, Hope—come on, you yip-yaps, we're pulling for you!

But a second phone call from Concho, after they had finished supper, brought Fibate back with slow footsteps.

"We're sunk, gang. Still tied, last of the thirteenth, but Spur has the bases full—and nobody out."

That turned the trick. Where nine tension-packed innings of baseball in ninety-five-degree heat had failed to wear down Sonora enthusiasm, the news that Spur was again going to slide through undefeated came like a leaden weight on the shoulders of everyone. Silently they filed out of the restaurant. They took their places in the bus, curled themselves as comfortably as possible, and tried to sleep.

No more stops were made. No more phone calls.

But just outside Sonora, when they had climbed the nearly one-seventy miles up the winding canyon road homeward, a strange glare of multiple headlights blocked the way. The boys sat up, rubbed their eyes, glanced at one another.

The bus braked to a stop. Into the glaring light between cars walked George Headrick, handsome, white-haired mayor of Sonora. Cap'n Al climbed out to meet him. The team followed, wondering.

"Welcome, champs!" the mayor greeted them.

Instantly two dozen automobile horns chimed a noisy confirmation. The players exchanged pleased glances.

Cap'n Al was the first to catch on. He grabbed Mayor Headrick by both coat lapels. "You mean, Hope did manage to beat Spur?"

"Sure! Didn't you know? Seven to six in fourteen innings. Boy, what a game! But never mind that—it's *you* we're craving to see! The whole town is up waiting. You're tied for first, boys!"

Again the din of many auto horns.

First place! Did you hear that, gang? First place—tied with Spur! Only two more to go: one a push-over at Vocant, day after tomorrow, then only Greenfield!

One of the wild celebrants grabbed Cap'n Al Carter. "How about giving us the day off tomorrow, Coach? We've earned a rest. We can whip Vocant, hands down!"

Cap'n Al produced a smile, but there was no uncertainty in the way he shook his head. "Practice to-morrow, as usual," he decreed. "Only, we'll start at two —one half hour early!"

But not even that gloomy pronouncement could chill their enthusiasm now. In first place, weren't they? On the top rung, after all these weeks! Another crack at Spur! Bring 'em on!

Chapter 12

STRANGE DEVELOPMENTS

CAP'N AL drove his charges at a furious pace the next day, desperately trying to whip the traditional bugbear of all winning high school teams: overconfidence. He liked the winning spirit, all right. He had built it. Demanded it. But the general air of cockiness that the coming game with Vocant was already in the Win column went far beyond the team itself. It saturated the very air about Sonora High School.

Beat Vocant?

Shucks—Vocant wouldn't have any more chance than a grasshopper in an anthill! Down in seventh place, weren't they? *Ninth* place, if they hadn't lucked out on Concho last Wednesday! And supposing they had beaten Concho—what of that? Concho was nobody!

Cap'n Al tried to stem the tide by pointing out that Vocant, besides beating Concho and Lakewood, had also whipped Mesquite only two weeks before. Mesquite had a good ball club.

Still, he couldn't swing the balance. It just wasn't logical for Vocant's one pitcher, a good little twirler for five innings, perhaps, to hold out against sluggers like Bill Burnham, "Slow Molassas" Smith, Chic Stahl, and Red Bailey over the full route. Why, they'd murder him!

Vocant was only ten miles down the canyon, so in view of the fact that Sonora was tied for first place, the school authorities went into a quick conference. They emerged with a decision to treat the student body to an afternoon off and a trip to the game. Noisy, confident students promptly took over the town.

Bronc Burnett spent Friday night in town with Fat Crompton, after the game with Vocant, and the two thoroughly exhausted boys slept until nearly eleven o'clock the next morning. They didn't want any breakfast. A neighboring cowman who had driven in for supplies gave them a ride out to the Burnett Ranch.

"I believe Dad's home for the week end," Bronc said, noticing a sweat-lathered horse that had recently been unsaddled in the corral. "He's been rounding up strays on Rock Mesa, so I didn't really look for him until Thursday or Friday."

"Things don't always turn out like a fellow expects."

Bronc threw a side glance at his companion. "I know what made you think of that."

"I haven't thought of anything else," Fat Crompton said grimly.

"Let's go inside the house."

"Yeah. Just as well."

The Burnett home was a low, flat-topped adobe building with a vine-covered porch rambling around the front and the sides. Bronc and Fat passed through a wooden yard gate, crossed the shaded porch, and entered the living room.

"Are you here, Dad?"

"Sure, I was just asking about you!" Heavy boot heels clumped from the back of the house, and a big figure soon filled the doorway. "Howdy, Crompton! Well, how badly did you beat them yesterday?" Big Jim Burnett clapped his huge left paw on Bronc's shoulder, reaching out his right to shake hands with Crompton.

Tears welled in Fat's eyes. He turned away.

"What's the matter?" Big Jim demanded of Bronc. "Is

154

that fancy coach still trying to make a pitcher out of you?"

"I threw the game—yes, sir."

"And you lost?"

"The full story is in the *Messenger*," said Bronc, indicating the morning mail, which lay unopened on their front-room table.

Big Jim Burnett soberly picked up the Sonora weekly *Messenger*. He tore off the wrapper, beginning to frown as he read:

VOCANT KNOCKS LOCALS OUT OF TITLE RACE

Position	Teams	Won	Lost	Percentage
1.	Spur	7	1	.875
2.	Sonora	6	2	.750
3.	Greenfield	6	2	.750
4.	Tatum	5	3	.625
5.	Hope	4	4	.500
6.	Vocant	4	4	.500
7.	Mesquite	3	5	.375
8.	Suerte	2	6	.250
9.	Concho	2	6	.250
10.	Lakewood	1	7	.125

Final games next week: Greenfield at Sonora
Tatum at Spur
Lakewood at Hope
Concho at Mesquite
Vocant at Suerte

While Spur was winning easily over Concho this afternoon to take a solid grip on undisputed first place, Sonora dropped a heartbreaker at Vocant when rain halted the contest shortly after the fifth inning. The score was 3 to 0.

It was a bitter blow to our lads, because they had just gone on a vicious batting splurge which had already netted four runs in their half of the sixth. Not only that, the bases were still full, with only one out, when the deluge came.

According to the rules, the score then reverted to the last completed inning.

Rain had threatened throughout the afternoon, and twice the umpires suspended play during brief showers, but by agreement of both team captains they kept banging away at each other until the final near cloudburst stopped things for good and all in the sixth.

Bronc Burnett, pitching for Sonora, started in promising style by fanning the first two batters and throwing out the third. But in the second they climbed on him for four solid hits, to the tune of two runs. They picked up another in the third on two errors, and a humpbacked single too far for Smith to reach behind first.

Meanwhile, Joe Palmer, a slim youngster with more heart that brawn, was managing to keep our lads away from pay dirt when the chips were down. Bill Burnham tagged him for a hefty two-bagger in the third, then saw Bailey, Losey, and Drover go down in order behind him. And in the fifth, Bill himself failed to come through, with Smith and Harrell vainly waiting on the paths after a pair of clean singles. His weak pop-up to the pitcher settled that.

But in the fatal sixth, just before rain flooded the park into a fish pond, Sonora suddenly regained full batting form —and more! The team batted completely around, having the little Vocant pitcher helplessly at their mercy. Then, as aforesaid, the rains came, and those runs weren't worth the paper it takes to write this.

The box score followed.

Big Jim Burnett studied it closely for a minute. Slowly the paper slipped from his fingers. His steel-gray eyes began to narrow. Suddenly he rose to his full height. He strode across the room to confront Bronc and Fat.

Mr. Burnett's manner brought Bronc immediately to his feet. "What's the matter, Dad?"

"That new coach of yours. What in thunder does he mean, still trying to make a pitcher out of you?"

"Gee, Mr. Burnett!" Fat Crompton interceded quickly. "Bronc pitched a beautiful game, considering—"

"That's just it: '*considering*'—always an excuse—every time he goes to the mound! Why, it's absurd! A young husky who can play the outfield and hit like Bronc—"

"Hit like me?" Bronc laughed mirthlessly.

"Yes—hit like you!" the big rancher snapped. "You got two hits out of three times at bat, didn't you? The paper says so! That's good enough for—"

"Aw, those two hits were both counterfeit! One was a bunt that I beat out, and the other was a nice, easy, looping bounder that any third baseman should have handled. But yesterday the field was muddy, and the Vocant man slipped and fell. So, really, I didn't deserve anything."

"He deserves credit for pitching a swell game!" Fat declared stoutly. "The paper didn't tell it all, Mr. Burnett, because Fibate Jones turned in the story. And—well, you know Fibate."

"What do you mean?"

"Well, the story didn't say anything about the orders Cap'n Al gave Bronc in the second inning, just after the first shower. Cap'n Al was afraid Bronc would hurt his arm, throwing a wet, heavy ball. So even at the risk of losing a game, he ordered Bronc just to throw 'em across the plate. No speed—no curves—just right over. He figured, even at that, we were good enough to whip Vocant. And we would have been, too, if that awful rain hadn't tipped the scales for those lucky jaspers! Now, through no fault of ours, we've lost all chance to—"

"Hold on a minute!" Big Jim Burnett interrupted. "Doesn't Spur have another game still to play, the same as you?"

"Yes, sir. With Tatum. But we don't believe in miracles!"

"It might not be a miracle for Tatum to win over Spur. At least, Tatum gave you fellows quite a tussle.

157

It looks to me like they might very possibly beat Spur."

A low laugh from Bronc drew their attention. "Sure Tatum is good enough to beat Spur! That means we've still got a chance for a tie, and a play-off!"

"After you beat Greenfield."

"We'll take Greenfield!" Fat declared. "It will be easier than driving nails in a snowbank, if Cap'n Al lets Bronc pitch."

Big Jim Burnett grinned sourly. "Young man, you're wide open for an argument on the last fifty per cent of that statement. But I'll pass up the chance. And I'm sure going to be on hand for that game next Friday."

"Good!" two voices chimed together.

Cap'n Al Carter "shot the works," as the old saying goes, in the Sonora practice sessions all through the following week. And when Friday afternoon finally rolled around, he was able to field a team that looked ripe for its best game of the season. Their hitting was sharp, their fielding clean and aggressive, and they seemed to have just the right mixture of determination and confidence.

Shortly before game time, while Greenfield was taking the diamond for its infield practice, Cap'n Al stood watching his three possible hurlers: Carson, Lear, and Burnett. Sweat streamed from them all, as each was putting everything he had into these final warmup throws.

"The usual batting order, sir?" Fibate Jones inquired, approaching the coach with his score book in readiness.

"Yes. No change."

"And Pitch Carson on the mound, of course?"

Cap'n Al frowned slightly. "I haven't made up my mind. Come back in two or three minutes."

"Yes, sir." Fibate hesitated. "Gee, fellow!" he said to Pitch Carson. "That hook sure was a beauty! You've really got your stuff today!"

"Get on out of here, before we jail you for lobbying!" Bronc Burnett growled back over his shoulder.

Bronc was sorry for the words, even as they left his

lips. But Bronc was certainly under a strain today. He went on with his throwing.

"Your control isn't as good as usual," Cap'n Al told him presently. "You're nervous as a horse with blinkers. What's the matter—the crowd again, now that you're back in front of the home folks?"

"No, sir! That rabbit ears stuff has been dead and buried."

Bronc wound up, and cut loose with a fast ball that hit the dirt in front of Crompton. He straightened to receive Crompton's return throw. At this point Fibate Jones plucked Cap'n Al's sleeve, interrupting. "The Greenfield coach has asked for our line-up. Shall I put down Carson and Yoder for the battery?"

"Yes," Cap'n Al decided. "I guess so. Burnett's control isn't as sharp as usual. You and Crompton stay here in the bull pen in case we need you," he told Bronc, then motioned the rest of the team to the Sonora bench.

The fireworks began early!

A pass to the Greenfield lead-off man and a bunt that Carson fumbled put men on first and second, with no-body down. And when the third-place hitter poled a healthy two-bagger scoring both runners, Wasp Dillon came at a trot with orders from the coach for Bronc to resume throwing immediately.

However, Pitch Carson survived the threat, and when Sonora came in to bat, they promptly started a little celebration of their own. When the first-inning smoke cleared, the score stood: Sonora 4; Greenfield 2.

The crowd gave their favorites a hand, as they raced back onto the field to protect their lead.

But Greenfield again picked up two runs in the second, and again Bronc Burnett was warming up with Crompton, when Pitch Carson staggered out of trouble. By strange coincidence, Sonora tallied another four in their half of the inning. Eight to four now.

"At this rate," Fat Crompton grinned, "we'll beat

them thirty-six to eighteen over the nine-inning route! A fellow couldn't ask for any more."

"Unless for Tatum to beat Spur this afternoon!"

The slug fest continued. By the end of the seventh, the score was fifteen to twelve in favor of Sonora. Several times the invaders had pulled up within a single run. Bronc Burnett, still down in the bull pen, had actually thrown more balls than Pitch Carson out on the mound. But always the Sonora attack had come through with timely hits to keep a margin that Cap'n Al Carter considered safe.

As Sonora took the field to start the eighth inning, Bronc's father came out of the grandstand to join him and Crompton along the left-field foul line.

Bronc spread a grin. "How do you like the game, Dad? You like hitting, so— Say, what's wrong?"

Mr. Burnett was frowning. "What does Carter mean?" he growled. "We need pitching out there—somebody that can choke off those birds. Why doesn't he put you on the hill?"

"Aw, we're winning the game. The score doesn't matter, I suppose, so long as we're ahead."

"It will matter, if you don't stay ahead! Why, they're hitting everything Carson can dish up."

"We're hitting their man, too. But where's your famous old theory, Dad? I thought pitchers were a dime a bushel, and it was only base hits that counted!"

"There are extremes both ways. What I'm telling you: that fancy coach has left his pitcher out there until he's shell-shocked. I don't like the looks of things, even if it is the eighth inning. And— Look there! What have I been telling you?"

A Greenfield batter had slammed Pitch's first throw straight back at him. Pitch knocked it down, then couldn't find it, and by the time he had turned around twice in trying to locate the ball, the runner had sprinted across first. Nobody down. It looked like another shaky inning ahead.

However, the next man grounded into a force at second, and the following batter flied out to Bill Burnham in center. The crowd breathed easier. Two away now, with a runner apparently stranded on first.

Their relief was short-lived. The next batter pumped a terrific liner above third base, which got past Peedink Harrell for an easy home run. Fifteen to fourteen now!

"Guess we'd better warm up some more," Bronc told Fat Crompton. "There's two down, and the sacks empty, but that last blow probably upset Pitch—especially, the way those wolves are howling at him."

"I wish they'd send you to the hill," Mr. Burnett muttered grimly.

"So do I," Bronc admitted. "But I'm trying not to think too much about it. Are you ready, Fat?"

For the "nth" time, Bronc began throwing to Crompton along the side lines, his back to the ball game.

Presently Crompton motioned him. "That's all! Drake just caught a pop-up foul. We can rest now, while our gang comes in to bat—and I hope it lasts an hour!"

Fat's hope was quickly shattered. The Greenfield pitcher threw only four balls to Sonora: Bill Burnham socked the first one squarely into the right fielder's hands; Red Bailey lined out to deep short; and after fouling one, Buck Losey was nipped by a step on a slow grounder to first.

Ninth inning. For the first time a one-run lead looked dangerously slim. Anything could happen this late in the game. You've got to hold 'em out there, gang! Got to hold 'em!

The crowd roared gratefully when Peedink Harrell raced in and made a shoestring catch, to retire the first man. The second batter also connected with one on the fat part of his bat, and again Peedink made the catch.

The roar up in the stands became thunder. Only one more to go, boys! Hold 'em! Hold 'em, boys—please!

But Pitch Carson walked the next man. And the one following beat out a slow twister to Smith. Two men on. A little bad luck on that one, Pitch. But it only takes one more! Let's hold 'em!

As Pitch toed the slab again, Fibate Jones suddenly went dashing out to the umpire. He said something, then the lanky sheriff-umpire took off his mask, called "Time out!" and turned to face the stands.

"La-adies and Gentlemen! Whoever comes out on top in this fracas will be tied for the Sapello Valley conference championship! Tatum has just put the handcuffs on Spur!

"Now, *play ball!*"

Play ball, nothing! A cannon shot would have been lost in the bedlam that followed—yelling, screaming, whistling, pounding one another on the back, and cowboy hats sailing out onto the diamond. The players themselves danced and jabbered like monkeys in a cage. Nor was the pandemonium confined to Sonora boosters alone. Greenfield was still very much in this ball game! Two down, but they had runners on first and second. Their clean-up man at bat. No, sir! They hadn't lost this game yet!

When order was again restored and Pitch Carson took his place on the mound, the noisemakers quieted. Once more a hush settled over the crowd. Again they could hear the players' chatter:

"Everybody alive! Make him hit to me, Pitch! Tag any base, gang! Any base—got a force on any base. . . . "

Pitch Carson delivered the ball. The crowd let out a horrified gasp as they saw it strike the Greenfield batsman on the arm. He dropped his bat, trotting off to first. Bases full now. A rangy left-hander came to the plate.

"Time out!"

"It's for us, Bronc!" Fat Crompton called to his battery mate. "Cap'n Al has yanked Pitch. Let's go!"

Together they walked to the plate. Fat Crompton dropped on one knee to begin excitedly buckling the first of two shin guards that Drake Yoder handed him, while Cap'n Al Carter linked his arm with Bronc's and started for the pitcher's mound.

"It's a dirty trick, shoving you into a spot like this," the coach said, "but you're the boy who can pull us through. Just keep your head and don't pay any attention to the wolves. A good pitcher has too much to think about to pay any mind to the crowd. You just play the game. Forget everything else, and just pretend you're on the practice field.

"How do you feel?" he inquired, then. "Got over your nervousness?"

Bronc held out his right hand. "Look! I could thread a needle!"

"That's all I wanted to know. Good boy! We've got a cinch. You'll come through for us!" Cap'n Al patted Bronc on the back, then hurried off the diamond.

The Sonora infielders came trotting in, clustered around Bronc, jabbering encouragement and nervously trying to pretend confidence. Their eyes alternately studied the waiting batter.

"Easy man, Bronc," said Captain Trail Drover. "He's hit three for five today, but two of 'em were scratches."

"Yeah, and Pitch fanned him once," put in "Slow Molasses" Smith. "You won't have any trouble. He'll be a sucker for that low curve of yours."

"Well, let's get started! What do you say—"

"Wait a minute!" Chic Stahl held up his hand, motioning them closer. "I've got an idea. Have you noticed that runner on second? He's one of those cocky little fellows, always dancing back and forth, taking a big lead. He'll be worse than ever now. With the tying run on third, he'll figure we won't dare risk a play toward second."

"You mean, Bronc should throw me a waste ball and we'll try to pick him off?" Fat Crompton inquired. He shook his head emphatically. "I'm *agin* it—probably wouldn't work, and we'd just have Bronc one ball behind the batter. I'm in favor of—"

"That isn't what I meant!" Chic interrupted hastily. "I want to use a trick play—one that Cap'n Al used to work in the leagues."

"What's that?"

"Well, when we trot back to position, Bronc is to pretend that he's forgotten all about this cocky little runner. Keep your back turned to second base, Bronc, see? That'll tempt him into taking a bigger and bigger lead, but don't you worry. I'll be watching him from over to one side. Then when the time is just right, you'll hear me shout: 'Let's play the batter, Bronc!' All right —when you hear that, you just stand there, with your back still turned, and count three. One . . . two . . . three. About that fast. Then whirl around and whip the ball straight for the base. Not to me—to the base! I'll be on the run, and I'll be there to grab it. We'll catch him flat-footed if—"

Pole Drinkwater's big voice interrupted. "Come on, boys! You're delaying the game!"

"Yes, sir!"

The infielders, chattering noisily, raced back to positions. Bronc took the slab. Quickly he threw his five warmup balls to the plate, putting plenty of steam behind the first four, and finishing with a fast-breaking curve that brought a grin clear through Fat Crompton's mask.

"Atta boy, Bronc! You'll do!"

The rangy, left-handed batter took his stance. Well back, feet together. Slowly he took a practice swing.

Straight, easy, horizontal. He seemed relaxed. There was Crompton's signal: low curve, outside.

"Good choice!" Bronc muttered to himself. "Believe I can handle this hitter. Might be better baseball than trying Chic's scheme, anyhow—if something went wrong— Gosh! Just supposing I did whirl and throw that ball clear into center field— This mob would—"

"Play ball!" the umpire ordered.

Bronc took his stretch, the ball now pressed with both hands against his shirt. Off in the distance, vaguely, he could hear the team:

"Everybody alive! Make him hit to me! *Let's play the batter, Bronc!* Everybody—"

The signal!

One . . . two . . . three!

Bronc spun around. He pegged the ball savagely to the base. Chic was there at a dead run, all right, and caught it. Sure enough the runner was trapped!

But instead of trying to slide back into a certain putout, he suddenly turned and started toward third base. "Go on! Run! Here's your chance!" he squawled to his teammate already occupying third. "Run for home— hurry!"

The runner on third had no choice. As the man from second was driven closer, forcing him off, he broke madly for home. But Chic Stahl was watching. And Chic was smart. He held onto the ball only long enough to ensure that the runner could not retreat back to third, then fired it to Fat Crompton, who was waiting at the plate. The runner tried to jostle Crompton into dropping the ball, but might better have tried to topple an adobe fence. He went hurtling through the air for his pains.

"You're out!" Sheriff Drinkwater bellowed.

The game was over!

In seconds' time, the mob was onto the field. "Let's carry the hero home!" voices squawked above the uproar.

Half a dozen of the crowd, too excited to realize what they were doing, hoisted Bronc Burnett up onto their shoulders. They started milling toward the side lines. Bronc, flushing with embarrassment, chanced to catch Fibate's eye over near the Sonora bench.

"Aw, nuts! You never even threw a ball to a batter!"

Chapter 13

THE INVASION OF SONORA

THE Superintendent of Schools and Cap'n Al Carter drove down to Spur early the next morning—Saturday. And shortly after eleven o'clock they telephoned back a message that lifted Sonora to delirious heights.

The one-game play-off would be on the following Wednesday. *At Sonora!*

There had been some controversy over this, they reported, because the only other meeting of the two teams had been at Sonora; but in view of the fact that Spur had played five of its nine games at Spur, while Sonora had only played four of its nine at home, the toss of a coin had decided. But Spur, a booming little city of eleven thousand as contrasted with Sonora's meager seven hundred, grimly promised that they would not be without rooters at the game. They would even bring their forty-piece band.

Plans began to take shape from the instant Mayor George Headrick hung up the receiver and relayed the news. By nightfall the town was at fever pitch.

And when a pep rally was scheduled for ten o'clock the following Tuesday morning in the high school gymnasium, townspeople and students packed the place to the rafters.

The team, grinning and self-conscious, were on the stage. Seated behind them were the superintendent, the

167

president of the school board, the mayor, four members of the clergy, umpire-sheriff Pole Drinkwater, and the commander of the local American Legion post.

The only person missing who should have been there was Cap'n Al Carter. Some said that the former leaguer had an inordinate shyness about speechmaking. At any rate, he had begged off and was supervising a group of volunteer workmen over at the ball park.

Fibate Jones, as student-team manager, was master of ceremonies.

After a short opening prayer, the rally got under way in a manner calculated to raise the roof: music, organized cheering, short talks by the school authorities and the mayor. Noisy applause greeted them all. Then the commander of the Legion Post was introduced. The same enthusiasm greeted him. He walked to the center of the stage.

"This isn't exactly the Christmas season," he began, "but I don't believe ol' Santa Claus will object to something we hope to do for this great ball team." Spontaneous applause met his words, "great ball team." He cleared his throat, waited for the noise to die down, then held up his hand. "As most of you know, the Legion is sponsoring a community barbecue and a huge bonfire tonight in honor of the team. But we are going even further."

He turned, half facing the team.

"Young men," he continued, "I am authorized to inform you that Sonora Post Number 178 of the American Legion—in the event you win tomorrow's game—will sponsor and finance your entry in the New Mexico State American Legion junior baseball championship tourney at Albuquerque. That's July twenty-first, and we hope—"

The ensuing blast would have put a steam calliope out of the running! It went on for several minutes, freely joined, now, by the shouting, whooping team members themselves.

"Holy cow, Bronc!" Fat Crompton howled in Bronc's ear. "Do you know what that means? Why, it's the biggest thing you ever heard of! More than a million boys all over the country played in the national junior tourney last year! Three hundred players now in the big leagues all got their start on these teams!"

"We've just got to wallop Spur! A trip to the state tournament—gee!"

Meanwhile, the Legion commander had taken his seat.

"Yeah, Sonora!" Fibate yelled suddenly. "Beat Spur! On to Albuquerque!"

Others took up the cry.

When they paused, from sheer exhaustion, Fibate began to introduce the various team members, one at a time. Uproarious clapping, whistling, shouting followed each, during which Bronc Burnett and Fat Crompton came in for equally generous shares, as their names were called. Bronc had been introduced as Rabbit Ears Burnett, but that didn't matter. Nothing did—except beating Spur. He was even trying to put the Albuquerque trip out of his mind, until they'd beaten Spur!

While the packed crowd slowly untangled itself afterward, the various local celebrities on the platform shook hands with the boys. Classes were ultimately resumed, but nobody learned anything that day, except more about baseball hysteria!

Cap'n Al gave the team a strenuous workout from two to four, and lectured them severely for their erratic play.

"You're already taut as a wet lariat!" he complained. "Nobody knows how much worse you'll be by tomorrow. For two bits I'd keep the whole pack of you away from that celebration tonight!"

He let them go, however, but with the stern admonition that they were all to be in bed, with the lights out, by ten o'clock.

But not even this satisfied the coach. About mid-morning on the day of the game, Bronc and Fat, along with four other team members, were summoned from a study-hall period to the principal's office. They found Cap'n Al there. Also the superintendent of schools. By twos and threes the rest of the team presently filed into the room. They eyed one another wonderingly, whispering behind cupped hands.

The principal motioned for silence. "Boys," he said, "your coach here, Mr. Carter, is deeply concerned with what he calls the 'carnival air' with which you are surrounded. Is that correct, Mr. Carter?"

"Yes," Cap'n Al responded. "I don't like it a bit. We're going to lose that game by twenty runs the way folks are getting our team keyed up. It would be different if we were scheduled for a football game, or boxing, or a cross-country run in track—you need the old never-say-die determination there. But it's sure death to a baseball team.

"I want my boys relaxed, loose, grinning—cocky, if you please. Why, look at them now! They're solemn as an amateur trapper getting ready to skin a skunk. There isn't a one in the bunch that could catch a baseball in a wash tub!"

The coach's droll way of putting things brought only short smiles to the circle of hushed, waiting boys.

"Mr. Carter has asked that you be excused from classes the rest of the day," the principal said. "Certainly we're glad to do it. You have earned it, boys. His plan, I think, is to take you out of town—"

"To Mayor George Headrick's home," Cap'n Al said. "The Legion has donated a truckful of army cots, and we're having them put in Headrick's back yard. You'll lie down, quietly, from ten to eleven. From eleven to twelve we'll go over our signals, rehash the mistakes of other games, and discuss how to play the various Spur batters. Fibate, be sure to bring your score book. We'll need the record of their hitters in that first game."

"Yes, sir."

"Two of the team mothers, Mrs. Burnett and Mrs. Crompton, will help Mrs. Headrick serve you a light lunch at noon. Afterward, you'll take another one-hour rest, then you should be ready to act more like a baseball team. Are there any questions?"

"Just one!" The superintendent of schools, a graying, kind-faced gentleman had a twinkle in his eye. "What do you plan to do about Slug Langenegger?"

The group laughed, breaking the tension.

Cap'n Al stroked his chin thoughtfully. "Slug is the most deadly batter, pound for pound, that ever grew up in the Southwest, but he's clumsy as a hog on roller skates, at any position in the field. Actually, his fumbles cost them the only two games they lost this year. So their strategy now, I hear, is to use him only as a pinch hitter.

"That means: any time they get a man, or two, or three, on base, he's almost a cinch to pound them in. Not a very pleasant thought.

"That's why," Cap'n Al concluded, "I want my boys to be better than their best, instead of merely better than their worst!"

"We'll co-operate to the limit! Your bus is waiting downstairs now, and Wasp Dillon will be along with the uniforms and equipment shortly after lunch."

Loitering students set up a cheer as the team went through the hallways, and every window on the street side of the high school was crammed with noisy well-wishers as the bus rumbled away.

The sun had never risen on a better baseball day than Sonora gave the invaders by warmup time that afternoon. Not a cloud in the sky and just hot enough to bring out healthy, limbering sweat on the players.

Spur hadn't been talking idly about bringing a crowd. They seemed to outnumber the home team by five to one, despite the fact that every cowboy, miner, and forester for twenty miles had ridden in to boost for Sonora in the play-off. The grandstand was filled an hour before game time, and when the teams had finished their batting practice, some thirty minutes later, automobiles were parked in a solid circle around the field. The Spur band, a gaily bedecked outfit in red, white, and blue, lent added zest to an occasion that would have been historic even without it.

Cap'n Al's "isolation ward" had done the Sonora team a world of good. Their hitting had its former reckless abandon, and in their infield workout they fired the ball with a carefree cockiness that had never looked better.

Meanwhile, Carson, Lear, and Burnett were toiling down along the third-base line with their catchers. Not one of them knew who would start; Pitch, it seemed likely, with the others ready to step in the moment he faltered. Or, it might be Lefty. He was at his best against left-handed hitters, and the Spur line-up contained four of them.

"It's only five minutes to game time," Fibate Jones presently reminded the coach. "Have you decided on a battery?"

"Yes."

Fibate opened his score book and adjusted the lead in his pencil. "Well . . . who?"

"Burnett and Crompton."

"Now, wait a minute, sir!" Fibate tucked his score book under one arm. All the color had drained from his thin, sharp-nosed face. "I've been a good helper all year, Cap'n Al," he began nervously. "I haven't butted into your affairs—not once! But on behalf of the school—on behalf of the rest of the team, who don't dare question your decision—I want to say a few words, right now."

"All right—say 'em!"

"I think you're making a mistake. It's just too huge a responsibility for Burnett—the biggest crowd that ever saw a game in Sonora—the noisiest—and the very same bunch that ruined him and his rabbit ears before. It'll be a dozen times worse today. Everything is against him. On the other hand, Pitch is a senior. He's been under fire before, and the crowd will not affect him. Besides, he knows the batters. Why, he'll tie them in knots! What do you say, Cap'n Al? It means so much to the boys—the championship, the trip to the state Legion tournament, the—"

"I've been thinking of the boys," Cap'n Al agreed thoughtfully. "This championship does mean a lot to them—to the town. To me, for that matter. It's the climax of everything we have worked for all season. You're right, we *must* win this game!"

"Then you'll start Pitch Carson?"

The coach shook his head. "Our battery will be Burnett and Crompton! Now get over to the bench, you fellows—all of you! You'll have two or three minutes to catch your breath, then we swing into action!"

The diamond was deserted, now. Spur had completed the infield workout, and a groundkeeper was smoothing the roughened spots around home plate.

Umpire Drinkwater's "Play ball!" sent Sonora racing to positions. Bronc Burnett took his lonely stand in the center of the diamond. The wolves began to chew on him immediately. Never had such a tirade broken loose in Sonora. The home rooters tried nobly to hand it back, but theirs was like a whisper in a whirlwind.

Bronc heard, of course. And it bothered him. It would have bothered anybody. Nevertheless, he kept his gaze so rigidly fixed on Fat Crompton behind the plate that the wolves couldn't catch his eye. He took his five warmup throws slowly, deliberately, putting plenty of power behind the last one. Fat promptly fired it to second. But Fat's peg was at least ten feet over Chic Stahl's head. The wolves immediately turned their venom on Fat.

That stung Bronc worse than when they had been riding him. When the ball was returned, ready now for play, he stepped down in front of the mound and beckoned to Crompton.

"What's the matter, pardner?" Fat was breathing rapidly, his face deeply flushed, as he came close.

"I was just thinking," Bronc drawled lazily, "did you ever hear the one about the tourist who stopped at a place in the Arizona desert for a drink of water?"

"No! What's that got to do with winning this ball game?"

"When the tourist had finished drinking," Bronc went on, "he looked around at the old-timer, and said: 'Say, doesn't it ever rain out here?' The old-timer scratched his head, sorta grinned, and said: 'Mister, we've got bullfrogs in this country that are five years old an' ain't never learned to swim yet!'"

"What's that got to do with this ball game?"

"Aw, nothing. I was just wondering if you'd ever heard it."

Fat grinned acidly. "With three thousand howling maniacs out here to see a championship play-off, you take time out to tell me a stale story!"

"It isn't stale! I thought—"

"Nuts!"

Fat Crompton whirled and stamped back to the plate. But when he took his position behind the batter, Bronc could see that the familiar Crompton grin was back where it belonged. The wolves wouldn't bother him now.

All right, let's get down to business. What's this little runt hoping for? What's he dreading?

The batter was left-handed. Stooped-over, like Peedink Harrell. He was holding his bat perfectly still, poised back of his shoulder . . . ready. Short, choked grip on the handle. Fat was calling for a fast ball, slightly inside.

Suddenly the Spur band began to play—a booming, noisy, discordant piece. Purposely raucous, Bronc knew. It nettled him slightly as he started his windup.

"All behind you, boy! Shove it in there, Bronc, boy! Make him hit to—"

"Strike one!" the umpire said.

The batter had not offered.

Fat snapped the ball back. "That's the way to go out there, Bronc! That's the way to go!" He signaled for a curve. Bronc gave it to him. Strike two! Two and nothing. "That's the way, Bronc! That's the way to go!"

Better waste a couple now. Might tempt him into swinging at a bad one. Even if he connected, it wouldn't go any place. Cap'n Al had once said that some big-league managers would fine a pitcher five hundred dollars for grooving one with a two-and-nothing count.

Bronc shot a fast one, high and inside. The batter leaned back, let it go by. Two and one now. Fat had been setting him up for a curve. There was the signal—outside curve. Bronc hesitated a moment.

Lead-off man—probably a smart, canny little fellow with plenty of baseball savvy. He wouldn't be expecting a strike this soon. Another waste ball, probably, then he'd be set for one. "I'm going to try for an outside corner," muttered Bronc. "Columbus took a chance—so will I!" He wound up slowly.

"Everybody alive out here, gang! Make him hit to me, Bronc! Make him—"

Bronc shot over a fast curve. Strike three—called! Sure enough, he had outguessed the Spur lead-off man.

But the little fellow had whirled on Pole Drinkwater, was arguing savagely. Half a dozen of his teammates came running out. The Spur crowd took it up. That hadn't been any strike! Too low, of course. Anybody could see that the ball was down almost in the dirt. Wide of the plate, too. A foot outside. Hey, get somebody to call 'em that can see!

The tall umpire-sheriff let them yelp for perhaps a minute. Then he pointed to their bench and calmly pulled out a big, old-fashioned silver watch. "I'll give y'all just thirty seconds to get back on the bench," he drawled. "Now, *git!*"

"You haven't got the nerve! This crowd will pull you to pieces!"

"Twenty seconds! Fifteen seconds! Ten —"

The Spur team raced one another madly for their bench!

Play was resumed with a stocky, heavy-set boy who swung from the right side of the plate. He seemed a little too far back in the batter's box, so they fed him an outside curve. It should have been a ball, but the batter swung at it. Bronc promptly fired a fast, straight one over the outside corner. His theory worked. Thinking it also would dart away from the plate, the batter had watched it go by for a called strike. Two and nothing. The hitter waved his bat nervously. Bronc could see him grit his teeth. Another curve—this time, too far out. Two and one. Suddenly Fat called for a fast ball, inside. Bronc nodded. Good stuff; he's been crowding closer to the plate with every pitch. We'll drive him back with this one, then switch to another outside curve. Bronc turned it loose.

A roar went up from the crowd as the stocky batsman, obviously expecting another curve, stepped forward and was hit on the leg by the pitch. He dropped his bat, limping off toward first.

"Never mind that, Bronc! Couldn't help it in there, boy! We'll get the next one! Make him hit to me. . . ."

The band blared out with another fast, noisy tune. The wolves, given a new lease on life, started heckling Bronc from the first-base lines. Then, above all other confusion, a familiar voice:

176

"Strike him out, Bronc! Whoopee! Here—let me show you what to throw him! Look here, son!"

Bronc Burnett fought a terrific battle with himself. Fought—and won! Though he would have given his right eye, almost, for a quick, reassuring wave of the hand, he completely ignored it.

Who was the batter? Another left-hander. Big brute, too. As he caught Fat's signal for an outside low one, Bronc saw something else. Pitch Carson was leaving the bench with Drake Yoder to warm up. Gosh! Did he look that bad to Cap'n Al? Bronc gritted his teeth and stepped onto the rubber.

"Don't forget you've got a runner over here!" Smith yelled from first. "Don't let him get too big a lead!"

"Hey, out there! Hey!" One of the wolves jeered raucously. "They tell me your old man got kicked off the school board!"

"He's never been on the school board!" Bronc wanted to snarl back, but he kept hold of himself.

"Everybody alive now, gang! Make him hit to me, Bronc! Everything in your favor, boy. . . ."

Ball one! Ball two!

The big lefty wasn't going to swing at an outside ball. Bronc was in the hole now. He'd have to come in with it this time. A low curve, right over, Fat signaled.

The batter drove a sharp grounder to Chic Stahl, playing considerably to the right of his usual position. Chic fielded it neatly, started to throw to second for a double play, then noted that Trail Drover had failed to cover the bag. Too late, he tried for the man at first.

Runners on first and second now. Only one down. Clean-up batter at the plate. He was a big fellow with arms like stovepipes and a vicious grin on his face.

"All my fault in there, Bronc!" Trail Drover called miserably. "I just forgot to cover on left-handers. But I'll even it up for you, boy!"

Bronc fed the big fellow a low, sharp curve. He swung and missed. They gave him another. Strike two!

A sudden, spontaneous outburst from the stands drew Bronc's attention to the Spur bench. The great Slug Langenegger had got up, was slowly swinging three bats.

"Slug can hit anything any pitcher can throw!" they'd said of him all season.

Bronc grunted under his breath. "We'll cross that bridge when we get to it!"

He looked to Fat for another signal.

Two and nothing on the batter. Crompton was calling for an outside fast ball. Bronc delivered it. But it wasn't outside far enough. The fellow lunged into it, connected on the end of his bat, and pounded a liner into left field. Peedink Harrell came running in, halted, then turned, and began to run furiously in the other direction. He had misjudged it terribly. The poke was good for two bases, and both runners scored.

The crowd went wild. Slug Langenegger wasn't needed—yet!

Down along the side lines, Bronc could see Pitch Carson hurrying his warmup throws. But Bronc stayed in. He cut loose savagely and fanned the next man on four pitches. Trail Drover threw out the last one, short to first.

Sonora came racing in for their half.

"Never mind that, gang! We'll get those runs back! Let's get a dozen. . . ."

Cap'n Al motioned Bronc to sit beside him. "A little bad luck, fellow. They shouldn't have scored on you."

"Thanks, coach!" And Bronc had never meant anything half so much in his life. He'd get to stay in!

The score stuck at two to nothing until the sixth. Spur had never threatened seriously again; one base on balls, a single, and a bad throw by Buck Losey had allowed three of their men to reach first, but these had occurred in separate innings and caused no damage.

Meanwhile, Bronc Burnett had given the strike-three dose to five more of them at the plate. The Spur pitcher, though still holding Sonora to a shutout, had been in constant trouble, but sterling defensive play by his teammates had continued to pull him through the rough spots.

Spur was a big team—rangy, fast, noisy, and playing with the confidence of champions.

In the last of the sixth, however, Bailey drew a base on balls for Sonora. Losey followed with a clean single over second, and Trail Drover beat out a bunt to fill the bases. Fat Crompton took two vicious cuts at the ball, missed them both, and then pushed a grounder to third. They got Bailey at the plate, but Crompton made first. Bases still full. One down now.

Bronc Burnett came to bat. He caught his signal: the hit-away

"Give us a pinch hitter!" he heard Fibate scream above the roar of Sonora supporters. "Put in Drake Yoder! We may not get another chance! Give us a pinch hitter!"

The home crowd took it up:

"Pinch hitter! Give us a pinch hitter!"

Bronc held his breath. He did not dare to look over toward Cap'n Al. Any slight move, or gesture, might tip the balance against him. And how he wanted to finish this game! Come on, you Spur pitcher. Hurry up, before they do take me out. Why doesn't Pole make him quit stalling?

Cap'n Al let Bronc hit. It wasn't anything to brag about—a fairly sharp grounder to short. Too late to catch the speeding Losey en route home, the Spur infielder elected to try for a double play. They caught Fat Crompton at second, but Bronc Burnett—running with the desperation of a scared antelope—beat the relay to first. Two outs now, but they had scored a run. *One* to two! Men still on first and third.

Peedink Harrell tried to catch them off guard with

a surprise bunt down third-base line, but it popped in the air instead, for an easy catch.

A scoreless seventh inning rolled past. Both pitchers had got stronger. Their teammates, too, were handling the ball with more dash and abandon.

Still two to one, as the last of the eighth came around. Chic Stahl was first up. He led off with a double. Atta boy, Chic! Now, come on, Smitty! Smith fouled an even half dozen, then waited out the Spur pitcher for a base on balls. The home crowd went wild as Bill Burnham strode to the plate. Out on the field the Spur team clustered momentarily around their pitcher.

Again the game was on! Strike one on Bill. Ball one. Then, unexpectedly, the slugging outfielder dumped a slow bunt toward first. He was off like a greyhound. He made it—the defense had been too deep.

Bases full! Nobody down!

Applause thundered from all around the diamond. The Spur team took a short time out, huddled in the center, heads down, cleated shoes pawing nervously at the dirt. Then, as if on signal, they suddenly turned and dashed back to position. Once more they were chattering and jabbering like blue jays, though it was lost on the yelling, howling mob in the stands.

Red Bailey took a called first strike. He lashed out at the next one, connected, and saw it go bounding straight through the pitcher's box. A hit—no! For a split second it had looked like a sure base knock, but the Spur shortstop raced over and speared it with one hand, right on top of second base. He dragged his toe across the bag, then whipped to first. A double play! But one runner had scored. Smith waited on third.

Tied up at last. Two and two.

The crowd was almost afraid to breathe, as Buck Losey stepped to the plate. Ball one. Ball two. Then he smashed one that scored Smith. Three to two!

Spur halted the game. Their coach sent in a tall,

gangling left-hander. His delivery looked awkward, but was good enough to retire Trail Drover on a pop-up to first.

Sonora took the field. The ninth! Leading three to two. One run had looked almost insurmountable, when Spur had held it over them. Now it was pitifully thin. The boys' tenseness showed in their chatter:

"Let's hold 'em Bronc, boy! Oh, let's hold 'em! Only three more to go, boy—we'll help you, if we can. . . ."

Maybe he wouldn't need it!

Certainly the first man went down in a hurry. Two strikes, a waste ball, then a vicious swing that missed by a foot.

"That's the way to go, Bronc, boy! That's the way! Make him hit to me. . . ."

But the next man poked one that took a crazy hop just before it got to "Slow Molasses" Smith. Smith fumbled. Mingled shouts and groans went up from the crowd. The shouts gained volume when the following batter hit to Losey. He, too, fumbled momentarily—then was a step late with his throw. Runners now on first and second. A squawling, howling mob stood up in their seats.

"Bucket" Baker came up for Spur. Baker, the big right-hander who always pulled away from the plate on his swing. He had been an easy out all afternoon.

But this time he refused to nibble at the usual ouside curves. The home crowd swallowed hard at Pole Drinkwater's "Ball four—take your base!"

The sacks were loaded. Only one down.

Again Bronc saw Pitch Carson hasten to the warmup area with his catcher. He dared not look toward Cap'n Al.

"Let's get two, gang! Everybody alive! Let's have a double play! Let's— Atta boy, Bronc!"

The batter had swung and missed. Pitching rapidly, lest Cap'n Al interrupt and take him out, Bronc had fired a terrific speed ball past the batter. Now, he could pause for a moment; that would give him a new lease! He eyed the batter carefully. Too anxious; it showed in his face. He'd strike at anything. They gave him a fast curve, outside. Strike two! Then strike three, in the same place!

The crowd thundered deliriously. Automobile horns blared from the circle, and men pounded one another on the back. Gradually the din lessened, only to begin again. And louder! Bronc followed the sound to the Spur bench.

An ominous figure with the shoulders and arms of a gorilla was slouching toward the plate, swinging three huge bats together. Now he tossed his two extra bats aside, pulled his cap down low above his bushy, beetle brows, and grabbed up a handful of dust. He wiped his hands on his pants, stepped into the box.

"Langenegger—hitting for Jernigan!" the umpire announced.

Chapter 14

THE THREE-TWO PITCH

TRAIL DROVER, captain of the Sonora team, promptly called for time. He trotted over to Bronc on the mound. Fat Crompton came hobbling out to join them, too, as did Stahl and Losey and Smith.

"Let's see what Cap'n Al wants us to do," Trail said.

They glanced toward the Sonora bench. But Cap'n Al wasn't even looking their way. The inference was obvious: he was leaving it up to the boys.

"Bases full!" Trail muttered. "Slug Langenegger up— they say the brute can hit anything a pitcher can throw! We might walk him, even if it forces in the tying run, and then go ahead and beat them later. If we don't, he's apt to pound in a whole flock of runs! What do you say, gang?"

There was a moment's tense silence as the group wavered. They stole uneasy side glances at the famed Spur slugger, leaning on his bat at the plate.

"Aw, nuts!" Fat Crompton blurted finally. "If it's up to me, I'd say: Pitch to him!"

"How do you feel about it, Bronc?" Trail inquired.

"I'm with Fat. If they get a run, let's make 'em earn it!"

The other infielders nodded agreement. One by one they slapped Bronc on the back, then trotted off to position, leaving him and Fat alone. The two stood watching the slugger.

"Got any ideas?" Fat wanted to know.

"Maybe."

"Then let's have 'em!"

"I was just thinking," Bronc said slowly. "Suppose we play this guy a little different. Let's give him three waste balls first. Then we can safely groove a strike. He'll let it go. Any ballplayer would; that's a fundamental. Then we'll give him another strike, not so good this time. A curve, maybe. With a three-to-one count in his favor, he'll probably let it go. That brings us to the three-two pitch. See what I mean?"

"I believe so!" Fat grinned, nodding. "Instead of giving the slugger three chances at strikes, to pick out the one he likes best, actually, this way, he'll have to risk everything on just one pitch. Okay! But what'll we throw him then?"

Bronc turned so the waiting slugger could not possibly see. Then he gestured stealthily with his fingers. "What do you think?"

Fat rubbed a grimy, sweaty sleeve across his big forehead. It was several seconds before he spoke. Then: "It won't work. The mob will just hang us both afterward —but count me in, pardner!"

He turned and trotted away.

"Play ball!" the umpire ordered.

Bronc stepped onto the rubber slab. Bases full. He paused to check his runners. They were holding close, obviously confident their burly pinch hitter would come through again—as he had all season.

From the bench, from the stands, from the cars, invading Spur was yelling, squawling fanatically. Sonora wasn't making much noise. Just sitting tight, staring out through half-seeing eyes at the drama about to unfold there, with the timbered canyon wall for a backdrop. They hoped, yet they dared not hope. Their very lives seemed to depend on that lone figure in the center of the diamond, the boy with the wide shoulders and the thin hips, who was getting ready to throw.

Bronc threw.

Ball one; so obviously a waste ball that the crowd let out a spontaneous roar that shook the diamond itself. An intentional pass coming up—anybody could see that! Bronc was going to walk in a run! The score would be tied!

The next two pitches followed quickly. Three balls on Slug Langenegger, who had begun to frown. He made no secret of the fact that he had wanted to hit.

Then Bronc began to unveil his surprise. Strike one! A blistering fast ball had cut right through the groove. Bronc took more pains with his next, a curve. Slug decided to go for this one. The crowd let out a stiffled roar as he smashed the longest, highest, hardest-hit ball ever seen in Sonora. But it was foul by ten feet.

The three-two pitch coming up!

Bases full—two down—Spur's last chance to keep the game alive. But what a chance! The big slugger looked ready. Bronc, himself, thought so. That bat looked wider than a scoop shovel. Slug's scowl, the glazed, merciless stare of a tiger.

As if moved by some mysterious common impulse, the crowd hushed, motionless.

All except one booming voice: "Strike him out, Bronc! Throw him some greased lightning!"

Everybody heard.

Bronc gritted his teeth. "Thanks, Dad!" he muttered. "That helps—more than you know!"

He took more of a windup this time. His right arm dropped back, his left foot came up, then his arm snaked forward. The ball was on its way.

But what a pitch!

It was a "slow ball"—a lazy, drifting, tantalizing floater that any seven-year-old kid should have hit.

Caught completely off balance, expecting a fast one that would sizzle, Slug Langenegger had already started his murderous stride toward the plate. Now he tried to check—tried to wait for the ball. But he had gone too far! The best he could do now was just slap at it with his wrist muscles. The ball popped back weakly, straight out in front. Bronc leaped forward and made the catch.

The game was over!

Slug Langenegger, himself, was the first to rush out and grab Bronc by the hand. "That took nerve!" said Spur's ace batter. "You'll go a long way, Burnett! Good luck to you, fella!"

Big Jim Burnett found Bronc with the rest of the happy, sweat-grimed team, grouped around the coach, who had raised them from mediocrity to champions. Big Jim's arm went around his son's shoulder.

"I've been expecting you, Mr. Burnett," Cap'n Al said, nodding to Big Jim, and coming out to shake hands. "I hope you're not too disappointed."

"You mean, over losing an outfielder?"

"Yes."

The big rancher's laugh boomed out above the surrounding confusion. "Listen! After today's game, I don't care what, or where, Bronc plays—so long as it's always on the pitching mound!"

The team joined Bronc and Cap'n Al Carter in a howl of delight. Big Jim was in the groove!

The next book in the Bronc Burnett series is called Legion Tourney, *and tells how Bronc, Fat, Cap'n Al, and the rest of the Sonora lads fight an uphill battle for the American Legion state championship.*